"Leg Befoɪ
A tale of greeɩ

Published in 2009 by New Generation Publishing

Copyright © Colin Goodwin

First Edition

All characters in this publication are fictitious and any resemblance to a real person, living or dead is purely coincidental.

April, Throttle Village, The Cricket and The Shenanigans Begin

"Brainless gits," muttered Albert Bradley.

He was removing the closed season's cobwebs and rust from some metal frames when a small group of people made their way past his house and up to the cricket pavilion opposite. They were hardly recognisable in the fading light, but Albert knew them right away, and although they were within nodding distance pleasantries were not exchanged. In fact he purposefully turned away and snarled as he wire brushed.

For most people the lighter nights and budding plants provide a feeling of renewal, a spirit of optimism with summer just around the corner but for Albert Bradley, April had other implications. His annual ritual had begun in earnest, and so, donning a well-used boiler suit, old gardening gloves and his third best flat cap, he dragged out two metal-framed mesh panels from his garage. He leaned them against the fence and pondered the awful job of getting them good enough to grace the front of his house.

"What's the point of having a smart house if you have to put these sodding things on it for six months?" he grunted.

His front garden used to be his pride and joy. He had won many trophies for his dahlias and roses at the local village fetes. He once thought about going to the county shows for the bigger prizes, but events beyond his control put a stop to that. It was as if the up and coming cricketers themselves had been treated with the same growth fertiliser that Albert used. Unfortunately for Albert, the result was that the players had outgrown the size of the pitch. These taller, heftier lads could slog the ball with ease up to the front of his house.

"Got to sort this once and for all," he added spitting out old bits of paint and getting angrier.

He had come up with all manner of guards to protect his prize flower heads from the ball, but after several direct hits, many near-misses and numerous arguments he considered it futile to carry on. So after one such incident, he had his lovingly nurtured strip of land paved over. Being an occasion too distressing for him to witness he stayed out of sight, and so as the workmen piled his previously nurtured plants into the skip and tamped down the slabs, he, sat in the kitchen hands firmly clasped around his favourite mug and scowled.

His wife, initially a supportive soul, but who more recently because of his moods, had come close to either braining him with a heavy object or just walking out was fully aware of his condition. She silently and dutifully provided sweet tea to guard against the shock but as he irritatingly slurped the tea through his teeth they both knew that it would take more than three heaped spoonfuls of sugar to offset the bitterness and resentment building up inside.

Throttle Cricket Club
An Emergency Meeting.

In the fading light, the silhouette of Throttle Cricket Club pavilion was quite imposing. Its large clock face high up in the eaves provided an appearance of significance in the sporting world. Unfortunately the clock was irreparably stopped. Clattered by a direct hit two seasons ago by a member of the opposite side who, point blank, and he had lots of support, refused to pay for a replacement. The other deception was that of the apparent solid grandeur of its fifties design. It was in fact a crumbling wreck. The mainly wooden structure had been starved of paint for as long as anyone could remember and in proper daylight the rot and peeling paint were obvious. Some locals said it made them feel at home, so the building developed into what it is today, a structure held together with string and rusty nails, where the doors are closed gently not slammed and no one dares open a window in case it falls out.

The assembled committee seated themselves down not knowing the reason for the hastily arranged meeting. John Appleby the club chairman had presided over many such meetings and had a well practised stance, his fat neck blended into the contour of his bloated belly where his trouser belt appeared to be strangling his waist. The thread of his waistcoat buttons was stretched to the limit as he coughed and cleared his throat. Then when all was silent, he peered over the half-round glasses perched on the end of his nose and in a sombre tone, apologised.

"Sorry to drag you here on a miserably cold night but summats cropped up. I got this, this morning from Sir Alfred T Bullock and Son. Thought I'd better bring it to your attention before somebody else does." He waved a single sheet of paper in the air to prove its existence.

"Better be urgent, this is my pool night up the shoot if it drags on," moaned Tom Deakin, the grounds man whose ruddy complexion confirmed that he had spent years facing the biting easterly wind and who was niggled at being dragged back after spending the whole day at the ground repairing the fence.

The chairman stared at him. "The sooner there's order, the sooner you find out, ok?" he replied raising his voice.

After a moment's silence John Appleby tilted his head back and focused on the letter moving the sheet back and forth to aid the clarity.

"Here we go then, from Sir Alfred T Bullock and son. I have to inform you and the members of Throttle Cricket Club that as laid down in the agreement, within any ten year period you have to win a trophy. It is now nine years since any kind of trophy or cup has been won. Therefore there is one season left to comply with this rule. After that the ground will be returned to the estate of Sir Alfred T Bullock and Son. Yours Roland Bullock".

The committee meetings had always been lively affairs with banter flowing either way, but on this occasion total silence wafted over them like an invisible blanket and took away their ability to speak, even if some mouths had dropped open.

Then Tom, never short of a word for too long blurted out.

"The scheming git wants to build on it, that's all it can be. Anyway, how come we didn't know this time bomb was ticking away?"

Heads turned to face Arthur Padstow, the secretary.

"Don't look at me," he defended himself. "I don't look at the frigging deeds from one year tut next. Besides I've only been here for five years. How the hell am I supposed to know what went on in sixty effing six?"

"Must be worth a fortune," said Fred Pickup the treasurer quietly.

The others turned his way.

"Why?" asked Janice, all round help, or as she called it "Dogs body".

"The ground, smack in the middle of the village, to a speculator it's prime building land... worth a fortune."

The committee looked depressed.

"Well thanks for that cheery note, point is what the soddin hell are we going to do about it?" appealed Tom.

"We'll start by keeping calm," advised Arthur as he took a final swig to finish his pint. He shuddered as the beer hit the spot then announced, "Then we'll do what we always do in a crisis."

He paused and looked around as they waited for words of wisdom, then continued.

"We'll organise another frigging meeting." He rose and pushed back his chair with the backs of his legs.

The noise, as the chair legs scraped the floor indicated his intention to leave, then as a parting shot he stared at the chairman. "Do it John, but this time, make it a big one, all invited, then there's no secrets. Everyone will know what the scheming Bullocks are up to, ok?"

Then he held his stomach, grimaced and belched loudly. "Crap ale and that heater stinks," he muttered as he left the building.

The others turned to look at an old bottled gas heater in a rusty casing. The yellow sooty flame that gave off little heat indicated that it was well past its best.

"Can you smell gas?" pondered Janice to the others.

The Bullock Household, A Frosty Breakfast

The Bullock's house, as the locals referred to it was a tall, detached Victorian dwelling perched on a raised plateau of land overlooking the village of Throttle. Its multi-level roof leading to outbuildings clearly indicated that beneath was a maze of rooms sufficient to house a very large family, and in times past, butlers and maids. Instead it housed one couple and their son. The breakfast arrangements at the Bullock household had deteriorated into a simple format.

Sir Alfred T Bullock, now wheelchair-bound since falling from a ladder, was arguing with his son Roland, who had taken over the day-to-day running of the firm.

"You've done what?" yelled Sir Alf, spitting half the contents of his mouth across the table.

"I've sent the cricket club what is in effect, notice to quit," replied Roland casually, and with a smirk guaranteed to wind his father up even further. "It's quite legal," he went on. "I've looked it up in the deeds, if they don't win a cup, and they won't, the land comes back to us. Easy." he said smugly.

"The land, the land, we don't need the bleeding land, it was my decision to give them the land in the first place, so it'll be my say-so when we want it back, ok?" Sir Alf emphasised his point by banging the table and in the process upsetting most of the coffee cups.

"Too late, letter's gone, oh, and by the way, if 'you' recall, 'you' gave me the authority to make decisions when 'you' put me in charge. Or had you conveniently forgotten that?" he pointed out with an air of defiance.

Lady Miriam Bullock, sitting at the other end of the table nibbled her toast whilst watching the back and forth of the argument. As she watched her face became increasingly etched with distaste.

"That's it, I'm off, I can't stand this bloody bickering, it's pathetic the way you two carry on. I've had enough. From now on I'm skipping breakfast," and she pushed her bowl of muesli away, tipping over the last remaining upright coffee cup in the process.

Miriam, as she preferred to be addressed, had dropped the "Lady" prefix ages ago on the basis it seemed a mite pretentious where outside toilets and coal sheds still existed. She had seen the relationship between them deteriorate, from at best frosty silences, to at worst slanging matches just short of violence. To add to this she had to witness the steady destruction of her dream home. She had been able to boast about the designer interior and country style roses round the door fittings, but now the home that was short-listed for an article in a glossy county magazine was being progressively wrecked by the ramps and lifts installed to accommodate her husband's wheelchair. She had been reduced to tears by having to stand and watch as the thirty pounds per roll wallpaper and the artistically scumbled doors and skirting succumbed to the treatment metered out by his careless driving. The scars along the wall bore evidence that he hadn't quite managed to stop himself careering out of control on his trips around the house.

"I see you've smashed another doorway, I'll be glad when you're bedridden and out of the way," she heartlessly growled.

"Sorry love, this new ones tecking some getting used to, mind of its own," he explained gazing at the controls.

"Don't call me love, you know it grates on me, anyway the only thing you ever loved was your soddin mill."

Sir Alf looked up as Miriam's eyes tightened with hate.

"Funny really, love life gone, mill nearly gone, you're wrecking this place quicker than we can repair it...well I'm going too," and with that she slammed the door behind her so hard it rattled the plates in an adjacent cupboard.

"Ungrateful bitch!" he shouted. He stared at the door for a moment then turned to Roland.

"As for you, cancel that soddin letter." There was a pause as Sir Alf's brain ruminated at Miriam's parting shot.

"What does she mean about the mill being gone, gone where?"

Roland stood up and backed away from the table.

"The letter's gone out, last week as a matter of fact, and the mill's not going anywhere, look,   got to go," he said hastily as he shut the door with a little less force than his mother.

Suddenly all was still, he sat in his wheelchair staring at the mess that was the breakfast table, then a voice from behind reminded him that he was not entirely alone.

"Finished, 'ave you Sir?" inquired Flora, the daily help, with a familiarity that made him smile.

In a split second, hearing that voice had changed him from being sad and miserable, to a person who believed that the day had more to offer, as he observed Flora retrieving a fork that had fallen to the floor.

"You all right?" she queried as she pulled at the edge of her skirt.

"Improving," he replied.

The Perkins House. A New Future?

Geoffrey and Susan Perkins and their daughter Alison had recently moved to Throttle Village with the promise of a new life provided from the earnings of his new job as Sales and Marketing Manager for the local Old Goat Brewery.

"You'll love it up here, the rugged landscape and fresh northern air, plus we get a lot more house for our money," he preached.

"Shops," Susan said when they were looking around the village, "where are the shops? I've spotted a chippy, a pub, and a paper shop, where are the proper shops, or do I have to walk around in rags like the rest of them?" she added sneeringly as a dowdily clad couple shuffled by.

"A bus ride away, you'll see, as soon as you get to know the place," he lied. He was getting used to lying, he found it easier than explaining.

Later, Geoffrey was standing on the doorstep surveying all he owned, or as he had been corrected by Susan "All that the bank owned," when he heard a curious scraping noise dubbed with cussing and swearing. So he peered over the fence to locate the source.

"Nice night," he said hastily as his new neighbour Albert Bradley turned and spotted him.

Albert looked up from his labours, specs of rust had stuck to the sweat on his brow and the red dust mixed with raindrops on his glasses amplified the anger in his eyes.

"Nice night, nice sodding night," he repeated, spitting bits of rust and waving the scraper as he spoke. "I'm scraping the shit off these, it's starting to chuck it down and you call it a nice night."

Shocked at the response he stepped back from the fence. "Sorry, didn't mean to be nosy, just wondered what you were doing."

"You've a set of these you know, back of your garage, better get yours painted and fitted to or your house will look like a knackered old pepper pot," he advised with an air of manic cleverness that disturbed Geoffrey.

"I wondered what they were for," he said, still puzzled as to their use.

They both went into Geoffrey's garage.

"See," said Albert pulling a cobweb encrusted frame from the wall.

"What do they do?" said Geoffrey becoming anxious.

"They stop the ball coming through the window," said Albert grinning

A voice from behind casually asked,

"What ball, whose window?"

They turned to see Susan standing in the driveway.

"Oh nothing," said Geoffrey trying to fend off a row, but he failed.

"Cricket club's ball, through your window," said Albert smirking. "You must have noticed, you are right in the firing line. From your living room window you can look right down the batsman's throat," he added, opening his mouth wide and pointing with his finger for effect.

"They'd never reach here…. would they?" Geoffrey posed.

Ten minutes later in the Perkins kitchen Susan ranted:

"You stupid, idiotic fool, nice to have a house near a village cricket pitch you said, turns out we are living 'on' the bloody pitch, prisoners in our own home on Saturdays. Our Alison will be killed instantly if she gets hit."

"Sundays and Wednesdays too," Geoffrey quietly muttered.

"We'll never be able to sell this house. No wonder he was keen to lower the price and give us the carpets," she went on. "That estate agent, he must have known. The devious… I remember him being pushy saying we had a bargain?"

Dumb struck, Geoffrey stood and listened.

"My mother comes on Saturday afternoons, what about her? She'll have to come in the back way, she will never believe this when I tell her. This is all your fault." She stared at him, then, in a fit of rage, ranted. "You absolute imbecile... what are you wittering about?"

"I've seen the fixture list, they play on Saturdays, Sundays and Wednesdays too," he said meekly.

Without hesitation she threw the contents of the mug she was holding at him. He stood, motionless and dripping as she strutted past him. Their daughter Alison who had been listening at the door approached him.

"Daddy," she said softly.

"Yes love, what is it?" He replied mopping his face with a piece of kitchen roll.

"What's an imbecile?"

His mouth fell open but no words came out.

Nasty Goings On, Throttle World Press

Arnold Bosworth, the recently appointed editor of The Throttle Flyer had aspirations to be the head of a tabloid journal, but so far his dreams had come to nothing. He continued to practice his banner headlines where he could but his approach to captions, some say over-stepped the mark and was not in keeping with a sleepy village paper. For example his banner headline reporting the simmering row between the church bell ringers and the immediate neighbours who brought out an injunction to have them stopped read...

"Gong bangers wrangle clanger"

However, the one that won him the prize for bad taste was the one about a jumble sale that raised money for a sick girl's operation

"Cash for trash pays for slash."

So when the news broke about the cricket club it was no surprise to see out side on the hoarding of the local newsagents.

"Cup boob club to go bust, sec' fails to keep abreast"

This headline had the other employees at the paper wincing, but they went ahead anyway.

His main problem was the lack of news.

"Martin!" he shouted, "what have we got today?"

Martin flicked over his journalist's spiral bound pad.

"Err, one lost cat, a fire in the rubbish bin outside the chippy, had to evacuate the café, big news that, eh?" he chuckled.

Arnold mused as he sucked the blunt end of his pencil, and then smiled.

"Roast cat menu shocks diners," he said as he wrote.

"You can't print that," replied Martin

"Why not?" added Arnold winking fitfully.

"Because it's not true," said Martin tilting his head.

"You can't prove its not true, can you...anyway, who says it has to be true?" Arnold reasoned. "And if anyone has the balls to complain, we print an apology on the back page. Simple."

"One day, one day it will all come crashing round your ears," Martin predicted under his breath. Then he spun round on his chair. "Are you going to the meeting?" he mischievously asked.

"Thinking about it...why?" Arnold edged.

"He's been on from the club, says he's going to pull your frigging head off, unquote."

"Best keep it down then," Arnold whispered.

Throttle Village Hall, 7pm, The Show Begins

The village hall had been full prior to the allotted time, partly due to concern relating to a village amenity, but mostly due to there being nothing on the TV, and there was a more than a slight chance of a ding dong.

John Appleby opened proceedings.

"Thanks for coming, nice to see such a large audience, so without further ado… we'll get on with it." He was just about to when a voice he recognised echoed from deep down amongst the audience.

"Resign, resign, resign," chanted a single voice from the back of the hall.

Everyone turned to see a spotty youth going bright red with the attention.

"I won't resign just because you were dropped from the second team, Craig Williamson."

Named, shamed, and now humbled, Craig slumped in silence.

John Appleby continued. "This is a serious matter, not helped by crap like this," and he held aloft a copy of The Throttle Flyer. "Tabloid journalism at its worst, and if the little shit who wrote it would stay behind, there's a few of us who would like a word."

Up until then Arnold Bosworth had anonymously sat at the back taking notes. On hearing what was to him praise indeed he wrote 'Yes' in large capitals as if he had won a prize, then he added the name Craig Williamson to his notes.

Unaware of Arnold Bosworth's presence John Appleby continued. "This is about the future of the club, a club that has been the mainstay of the village, where all classes of folk can play as equal."

In the audience eyeballs rolled back and stared at the ceiling as he slipped into Winston Churchill mode. Then he paused for a moment, took hold of the lapels of his jacket and taking a deep breath.

"Where men are men and..."

"And women make the teas!" shouted a woman from the back of the hall.

He raised himself onto his toes, lifted his glasses and peered to where he thought the comment came. The ripple of laughter beginning to influence the audience indicated he should abandon his speech

"Over to you, Mr. Padstow," he sighed and passed over the microphone.

On receiving it Arthur tapped the end and blew on it. "Can you hear me?" he inquired.

The audience groaned with embarrassment.

"Bleedin' Laurel and Hardy... get on with it!" shouted an exasperated man at the front.

"Aye well, the options are limited," Arthur informed the now restless gathering.

"We either win something and the status quo remains, or we don't and it becomes a building sight... and we don't want that do we?" he posed.

The audience began to mumble with indecision.

"Be nice to have a new house, don't like cricket anyway," a lady said in a shrill voice that amused the people sat close to her.

Arthur put his hand over the microphone and turned to the others. "Jesus" he blurted out. But his hand wasn't able to prevent the remark being broadcast round the room.

"He won't help you,"came a comment amidst the raucous laughter.

At the back of the audience three men were quietly smiling at one another.

"Piece of cake, easy peasy, the words a piss-up and brewery come to mind," confirmed Joseph Lagg the local estate agent to the two Jakeson brothers at his side who were beginning to wonder why they were there.

John Appleby took hold of the microphone. "Order, order can we have some ush?" He said spitting on the front row in the process.

To ensure complete silence he waved his arms as if flagging down a car.

"We have an announcement. In order to help us with our predicament we have enlisted the help of a professional, but no ordinary professional. On your behalf we have called upon the very able Mr. Benjamin Saxon, a big lad from Jamaica."

Screwed up faces in the audience suggested a lack of familiarity with the name.

"Well, not exactly from Jamaica, Leeds to be precise, well he lives in Leeds at the moment, to be honest we don't know where he comes from, actually," he added, looking for support from the others, but none came.

"Anyway" he shouted regaining his thread.

"But it'll cost, and as the cricket club has nowt, we were hoping that you, the people that this club serves, will either dig in your pockets and donate a few quid, or come up with some fund-raising ideas."

The noise of mumbling and chairs being scraped back was deafening. The moment he mentioned the word 'donation', people started to leave.

"Before you go, are there any questions?" he hastily added.

A giggly girl put her hand up.

"Yes love," he patronised.

"How big... is big?" she said unable to control her laughter.

"Six feet six, and hands like shovels," he replied puzzled as the audience fell about.

"That 'is' big," she enthusiastically confirmed.

Arnold, still with his head down scribbled furiously. "New pro excites nympho," that's the back page done," he mused. At the bottom of his page he scribbled, "Bitter young man," next to Craig Williamson's name.

Old Goat Brewery, Geoffrey's New Career?

Geoffrey Perkins arrived at the gates of his new employer. He gazed at the somewhat dilapidated facade that revelled of times past, "SUTCLIFFES' PIES AND PUDDINGS ARE THE BEST." A more modest plastic sign bearing a goat's head indicated the present use of the building.

"What the hell have I let myself in for?" he sighed fighting back the desire to head off back down the M1. He entered the dimly-lit office through a door marked "MEAT DELIVERIES." His heart was sinking fast and he was just about to call it quits when a voice behind him blocked his escape.

"Welcome, welcome" said Anthony Dawes owner of the brewery. He put a too familiar arm around Geoffrey's shoulder and went on.

"It might not look much but we like to call it home," added Anthony as he led him towards a plastic topped desk.

"Home...yes... home," Geoffrey muttered.

"Now then, I've got a busy schedule this morning, we are testing a new batch, so you have a shufty round with Jonathan here then we'll have a meet, Is that ok? About half ten in here."

Geoffrey stood to shake hands with a young man who looked like he was employed for his brawn rather than his brain.

"Meet, in here, coincidence that," he replied but the joke was lost. Geoffrey wandered around the brewery savouring the smell of the hops and barley. He wasn't a brewer, neither did he understand the complexities of all the pipe work and vessels. He just liked the taste of beer. Later, they sat at the table in Anthony Dawes's cluttered office.

"It's quite simple really, we have to sell more beer. The other bloke, the one who died, started a scheme where we sponsor all the local cricket clubs. Every player who scores a six or a four gets a free bottle of 'Owd Tup.' Then we hope they like it so such they get it put on permanent behind the bar. So it's up to you to finalise it before the season starts."

"Owd Tup, fine," said Geoffrey beginning to think he was on a different planet.

"Just one thing?" queried Geoffrey. "What did he die of?"

"His liver packed in," replied Anthony.

"Right," sighed Geoffrey putting two and two together.

Geoffrey explained the strategy to Susan that evening.

"So let me get this straight!" she shrieked. "You have to go round to that cricket club and suggest that every time they put our windows in, they get a free pint!"

Before he could explain, she ran up stairs and locked herself in the bedroom.

Laggs Estate Agents, Just Another Day?

Susan, who hadn't slept, and still hadn't calmed down, entered the premises of Joseph Lagg Estate Agent.

"Can I help you madam?" said the receptionist in a voice which really meant: can't you see I'm in the middle of reading my magazine, and you are disturbing me.

"I need a word with Mr. Lagg, if that's possible?" said Susan sharply.

"I'll see if he's available," replied the secretary. She spun round on her chair and disappeared into the back office.

"Lady to see you Mr Lagg."

"Can't you deal with it Julia," he replied without looking up from his crossword.

"Four letter word for tug...pull?" he mused.

"Jerk, "she said, in a low voice.

He scowled at her.

"Look, she's asked to see you personally."

"Ok, ok, just give me five minutes."

Julia returned to her desk and her magazine. "He will be out in a minute, Mrs..."

"Perkins," said Susan responding to the pause.

Moments later: "Mrs. Perkins, how can I help you?" he asked patronizingly.

"You can start by getting me and my family out of that house that you fraudulently sold us."

There was a pause as he contemplated the term. "Fraudulently, you say," he repeated as a young couple entered the shop.

"Yes, fraudulently, F, R, A, U...." she dictated.

"Yes, yes, I know how to spell it thanks," said Joe trying to keep his voice down.

"You sold us a house fraudulently by not informing us of the potential dangers of living there," she added volume for effect. She turned to the couple who were standing near the door listening.   "He did you know, I wouldn't buy a house off him, he's a con man."

The couple turned and left without shutting the door.

"And what's more if you don't come up with something, I'll spread it all over town about what you've done. By the time I've finished you'll not be able to sell a dog-kennel let alone a house." Susan felt as though she had won the first round.

"Come in the back and let's see if we can resolve the matter, coffee?" he said peering over her shoulder, but the day's first potential customers had gone. He beckoned her through into his office then paused and turned to his secretary.

"Two cups of coffee Julia, and wipe that smile of your face or its back to the job club. Take a seat Mrs. Perkins." He held out his arm towards an inferior typist's chair compared to his own armchair style.

She immediately spotted the differential, and set about him.

"I can take you to court you know and get damages, reimbursement, compensation, restitution and reparation," she said making it up as she went along, having spent the night reading, 'How to Sue and Win.'

"Mrs. Perkins, what's wrong with your house?" he asked patronisingly as Julia rattled in with the coffee.

"Our house is under siege during the cricket season, and if one of us gets killed it will be your fault because you failed to advise us of that fact."

Julia tried hard not to smile, but Joe noticed the corners of her mouth twitch.

"That will be all, Julia."

"You won't get me to admit it, it's that bloke you bought it off you should be suing," he said testing her out.

"He's abroad, somewhere, but as the go-between you should have told us of any potential danger," she responded sensing the upper hand.

"Now look," he rounded.

"You got that house cheap, very cheap, plus all those carpets and fittings." Then he paused. "But if it's any consolation, you, we, that is, could sell it for a quick profit." He then considered he'd said too much. I, I can't say any more," he stuttered. But you'll be grateful to me, just you see."

"How?" she probed.

"I've told you, I can't say any more."

"You'd better be bloody right or your name will be shit, do you hear," she said, causing him to sit up again. Next time I call... you'd better have some answers," she stared icily at him, stood up, and walked out.

Lunch time, A Meeting of Sick Minds

The local pub had been taken over by the Old Goat Brewery Company who immediately refurbished it to look even older. They removed all the original fittings then replaced them with pseudo old pub furnishings. To some of the locals who previously resolved never to set foot in the place again they said it was a perfect example of 'Fixing something that weren't broke in't first place'.

In the back room, Joseph Lagg was relating the earlier episode with Susan, to Roland Bullock.

"I'm telling you this woman's trouble, she will ruin me if we don't do something," he blubbered.

"Well we are doing something," Roland reassured softly, but then within a split second, turned.

"You didn't tell her anything did you, if I find out that..."

"No, no, nothing," stuttered Joe, clearly shaken by the threat.

"Don't give me that, you lie for a living, what have you said?" Roland hissed.

"Nothing, honest, well, only that if she hangs on she will be able to sell her house at a profit."

"Are you sure you didn't say any more?" probed Roland.

"Absolutely."

"Look," said Roland returning to his previous temper.

"All you have to do is make sure they have a shit season, shouldn't be too difficult, they have one every year."

They grinned, and then Joseph went serious again.

"But now they've got this new pro, this big black lad, hell of a reputation, they're all on about him, specially the women, he were over at Dabbington last year."

"Right," interrupted Roland, "Sounds like he puts it about, so you go over there and see if he caused any bother, bound to have upset some bint. You know the old saying 'Hell hath no fury like a woman who's been two timed.'"

A sickly grin came over Joseph's face that indicated he hadn't a clue what Roland was on about, but didn't like to say.

Throttle Cricket Club Meeting, Some Answers?

After the usual chitchat, the meeting got underway. Arthur Padstow read the secretary's report.

"I have to report Mr. Chairman that we've had several offers of ways to raise money, some good, some not so good, and one or two physically impossible... for me at least."

He held aloft a scrap of paper. "This one says it would be best to turn this place into a strip club, says it's full of tits already, might as well be proper ones."

The dirty laughs instigated by his statement were brought to a halt by a booming voice.

"Mr. Chairman, can this meeting be brought to order, I thought we were here to have a serious discussion." Clearly upset by the smut, Janice rummaged in her handbag for a tissue.

"Can we have a bit of order here gentlemen," said John, wiping the tears of laughter from his eyes.

"Arthur will you carry on," he grinned.

"Yes, well, err, another says we could set fire to the club and use the insurance money, could be something in that, what do you think, nice holiday out of it as well?"

"Are you serious or what?" responded Tom.

Fred Pickup, who felt his reputation was at stake, butted in. "Mr. Chairman, can I just point out that if there are any more references to immorality, unlawful acts, fraud etc. then you can have my resignation here and now."

"Now see what you've done," said Janice angrily glaring at Arthur.

"There will be no more references to fraud or any wrongdoing, will there Arthur?" added John

"Err... no" he said remorsefully.

"Karaoke nights are popular these days," said John hastily changing the subject. "Charge an entrance fee, put a few pence on a pint, and you've cracked it."

"I like that idea," said Janice beginning to smile." It's a while since we had a sing-song, be good for the community, we could put on a hot-pot"

"I don't think you understand what a karaoke is, do you Janice?" intervened Tom.

"Course I do. It's where we all get together and have a sing-song, I think it's a wonderful idea." she smiled.

The others smiled somewhat falsely back at her, then Tom with a grin added, "It'll give us chance to show off the new black pro, they can see what we need the money for. Mind you, we'll have to get some fresh beer in they'll never buy this crap."

As if to prove the distaste of the beer he produced a belch that not only shakes the rafters, but disgusts all present.

"Mr. Chairman," interrupted Janice. "I have to take exception to the terrible reference, 'The new black pro' It's offensive and racist, Benjamin is a gentleman which is more than can be said for some folk round here."

"Point taken, you'll have to be more careful Tom, we can't go round upsetting people, not right now."

"Sorry Janice," apologised Tom, putting on a pained expression as he patted his bulging stomach. "Gas, terrible gas," he added for effect.

There was a momentary pause as the committee pondered his words, and all were grateful when another member changed the subject.

"Can I have a word Mr. Chairman," interjected Fred Pickup formally raising his hand.

"Carry on."

"Thank you Mr. Chairman, I have to point out to the committee that a karaoke night is not going to pay for all Benjamin's expenses. We still need a minimum of six grand just for his wages."

The phrase six grand gets repeated around the table, each time with added emphasis.

"So we've still a lot of work to do. Mind you now that he is lodging with Janice we don't have to cough up for his digs."

The rest of the committee cynically stared in Janice's direction.

"Gentleman is he?" said Tom avoiding her gaze by inspecting the murk in his glass.

Tom Deakin Cold Calls The Brewery

"Hello there, my name's Tom, I'm from the cricket club up the road and I was wondering if you could help us out?"

Anthony Dawes could not believe his ears. "Come in, come on in... fancy a pint?"

Tom could not believe his ears either. "A bit early, but go on," he replied as though they were twisting his arm.

Moments later he held aloft a foaming glass straight from the barrel and was so taken with his good fortune that he had to blink to make sure he wasn't dreaming.

"We call it Old Goats Horn, what do you think?" grinned Anthony.

"Sodding hell that 'is' strong," he replied, exhaling as if he had consumed something peppery.

"Only supposed to have it in halves by rights, seven point five, comes under the heading of extra strong ale," Anthony advised.

"Is that seven point five on the soddin Richter scale," he said draining the glass.

"We have weaker ale, a three point nine, for the ordinary punters…. like to try it?" offered Anthony.

"Never been known to refuse, what's this called, Ram's Bollocks?" he replied jovially as the alcohol relaxed his decorum.

"It's 'Old Tup'... play on words, head banging stuff, took us ages to come up with that," he proudly boasted.

Tom finished his pint. "This'll do fine, don't want them getting pissed too quick, or they'll not be able to buy no more," he cackled. "Could I test one more Old Goats Horn, just to make absolutely sure?"

"Aye but be careful, it'll creep up on you," warned Anthony.

Ten minutes later, Anthony arrived back with Geoffrey to see Tom mellowing nicely.

"I'd like you to meet Geoffrey Perkins, our Sales Managing Director."

Geoffrey raised his eyebrows when he heard his new title. Tom looked in his direction but couldn't focus any more.

"Too strong for't punters," Tom confirmed, slurring his words.

"Give us hand to take him round back till he sobers up, it's bad for the trade leaving him here."

Karaoke Night, A Good Do?

The clubhouse was to have been given a coat of paint for the 'Karaoke and Meet the Pro night,' as it was billed. But the committee decided on low wattage lighting instead.

The attraction of the 'large coloured gentleman' as Tom was instructed to address him had ensured a good turn out which unfortunately threw up other issues.

"Beer's going down a treat," grinned Tom, feeling vindicated about the choice.

"But whatever you do, don't put the barrel on that's in the back, its a little stronger and for a very special occasion," he instructed David, one of the players who was helping out behind the bar.

Eager to make him feel at home, Tom approached Benjamin with a foaming pint.

"Here, get this down your neck, careful though, a few of these and you won't know what day it is."

Tom watched in amazement as Ben's huge hand wrapped around the glass and he literally poured the beer down in one go. "Deeeeelicious, does it have a name?" he posed.

"Well err, aye, 'Old Tup.' Couple of these and you'll tup anything."

"Then well have to put it to the test" he said letting his accent drag the maximum from each vowel.

His group of admirers, eager to please, fell about in affected laughter.

"I've heard you don't mess about," chirped one of them.

"Right," he drawled, "Youse gotta be as slow as a stopped clock but as hot as mustard."

There was a pause as they worked it out. A lady who was ear-wigging his comment grabbed the bar rail for support. David the helper was enjoying life behind the bar until the bitter pump began to emit only froth.

"Tom, help, beer's running out," he shouted over the heads of the mass of people holding empty pint pots in the air.

"Funny feeling this would happen," Tom mused as he made his way toward the cluttered little room behind the bar amusingly called 'The cellar.'

John Appleby, who was doing a spot of circulating at the time, spotted the concern on his face.

"Alright?" he inquired.

"Na, beer's going down faster than I thought, only one barrel left."

"So what's the problem?"

"The one that's left is a bit stronger that's all, I was saving," he broke off his sentence to choose the right words. "For a special occasion," he went on.

"Aye like cutting the grass, we're not bleeding daft you know." He said knowingly

"It'll have to go on, this lot will go mad if we run out," he added with concern.

"Ok, but we'll have to warn them, this stuff is soddin lethal."

John addressed the assembled guests from a makeshift stage. "Ladies and Gentlemen can I have your attention please. I'd just like to thank you for your attendance tonight and for making this a great do. I hope you have all now met Benjamin and had the opportunity to find out what a nice chap he is. I know he's already got his eye on one or two of you young ladies."

The committee and most of the audience cringed at his comments.

"He hasn't a soddin clue," Tom whispered to Arthur Padstow.

John, unaware of their anxiety, plodded on with his speech. "I would also like to take the opportunity of advising you that the ordinary beer has run out, and we are having to put on the emergency barrel. Old Goats Horn, it's called, for some reason. Problem is it's twice as strong so we're only serving it in halves... and I'm afraid it's twice the price."

Then as a hasty after-thought, "Oh, and before I forget, could you put your hands together for the ladies who organised the pie and peas, thank you."

John's plea for recognition of the ladies' efforts went unheard as the majority of the audience rushed towards the bar, whilst at the same time complaining about the cost.

The Results Of A Good Night's Work

Next morning at the cricket club, Arthur and Tom surveyed the damage.

"Don't tell me I didn't frigging warn you, it's like a plane crash, bodies everywhere, all over field, up the frigging sight screen, some idiot tried to get the bleeding roller going, I tell you, we'd have had fatalities if they'd succeeded." He glanced across the pitch, to where a small white car pulled up on the road. "That's all we need, PC sodding plod."

The local constable adopted the approach of a man whose peaceful Sunday morning had been disrupted.

"Judging by his face he's a bit hacked off," whispered Tom. He stood next to them and silently surveyed the scene, then turned back and stared at them.

"We've had complaints about the racket from three miles away. One bloke said he heard 'My, my, Delilah, six times, said he used to be a fan of Tom Jones, not any more. You've upset the whole neighbourhood, what's going on?"

"Bit of a welcome party, meet the pro," said Arthur.

"Goats Horn" replied Tom, "I told em not to."

"Don't take the piss," said the PC leaning so far forward that their noses touched.

"No, Goats Horn, it's a beer, only it were a bit too powerful for the locals, I'm afraid some of them got carried away."

"Some of them, some of them!!" repeated the PC in such a tone that indicated that he was not too pleased. Then went on. "All of them I'd say. This is a peaceful village, quiet, know what I mean, so don't you go wrecking it with your soddin sheep dip."

"Goats Horn," Tom politely corrected him.

"Whatever, be warned, comes under the heading of running an unruly house, causing a disturbance, an affray, not to mention drinking after hours. They could throw the book at you, all of you, all the committee, behind bars, sowing bags, eating porridge, sleeping with queers, for the rest of your natural, be warned." The PC turned and walked to his car, smirking as he faced away from them.

"Porridge is alright, not keen on the rest," laughed Tom.

Half way across the pitch the involuntary heaving noise emitted by another ashen figure throwing up against the clubhouse wall made the P.C pause, but only momentarily.

Just Another Day At The Bullock Household?

The breakfast remains had been cleared away and Sir Alf was getting himself psyched up for his new pastime, aptly named "Find the lady." A game conducted within the confines of the house and with the primary objective of giving him a purpose, not to mention easing the boredom.

Still not having come to terms with his semi-confinement after a lifetime of constant activity, he had decided that the parts of his body that were still functioning should remain so, and so this work-out for his arms and mind had been invented. The rules were similar to hide end seek. Flora had five minutes or so to hide then Sir Alf has then to find her within a certain time, usually half an hour.

Unbeknown to Lady Miriam, this pastime was the primary cause of the increasing damage to the interior of the house as Sir Alf raced from room to room with the clock ticking.

It was rare for Sir Alf to find Flora within the allotted time, but on the occasions that he did it caused them both to end up laughing out loud. As they got to know each other better, they found they could talk quite openly to one another. As the weeks went by they became quite close, a fact that confused him no end.

"All new ground to me," he would ponder out loud after she had gone home. Then one day after he had failed yet again to find her, she really put the wind up him.

"You know," she queried purposefully staring through the window so as not to catch his reaction, "We can spice this game up a bit if you like," she added quietly with more than a hint of embarrassment.

He cleared his throat "What do you mean, spice it up?"

Flora started to blush. "Well, I'm a bit short of cash, and you must be a bit, you know."

"A bit what?" he questioned.

"You know, short of the other."

"And how have you come to that deduction young lady?" said Sir Alf, a bit put out.

"Well it's obvious, the way you two carry on, can't be much love between you."

He stiffened in his chair "You are putting more than two and two together and assuming the worst." Then he pondered, "I have to admit, s.e.x seems a thing of the past these days," he sighed, spelling it out. Then the frustration got the better of him.

"It's only my legs that are useless you know, rest of me is ok."

"Hey, you don't have to convince me, I'm the one who picks up the forks every morning."

Sir Alf looked down. "What a bugger...but how did you?"

"No problem."

"So what were you thinking?"

There was a pause whilst Flora summoned the courage to speak. "Well... I go and hide, as usual, and if you find me within the time then, well... you know," she stopped and turned away.

"And if I don't find you, what then?" he asked.

"You give me ten quid," she added quickly.

"Ten quid, you must joking!" he shouted.

Flora looked shocked.

"Nothing less than twenty five," he grinned.

Her shocked expression gave way to a wry smile.

"Till tomorrow then," and she winked at him.

He awkwardly winked back.

As she walked down the drive he watched her from the doorway.

"Haven't felt like this in years," he told the empty house as he turned and shut the door.

"Feel like a kid on a first date."

He clicked on the kettle in the kitchen and pondered the decisions of the past hour. The possible consequences kept going round his head. He stared at the kettle as the steam began to pour from the spout.

"I'll be in bleedin' hot water if this gets out." His thoughts went round in circles. "What the hell have I gone and done," he confessed to the teapot. Then as he dunked his digestive he looked up the walls and around the ceiling, "What's to lose?" he mused. "Sod all," he concluded as the end fell off his biscuit.

Yet Another Cricket Club Meeting

Janice, stony faced stood outside the door waiting to be let in, she purposefully looked the other way as Arthur approach pointing the key towards the lock, as he opened the door a waft of disinfectant fumes hit him.

"Bleeding hell what's that?" he remarked, as his eyes started to run.

"It's the result of all my cleaning," barked Janice.

They left open the door and opened the windows.

"Now then, will anyone second the minutes of the previous meeting?" The chairman looked round.

"This is a farce, there's only four of us, we'll be here all night," said Tom, gesturing impatience by folding his arms.

"You have to observe the rules of running a meeting," said Arthur haughtily.

"I know, rules, is rules, just get on with it," said Tom reluctantly raising his hand.

John nodded towards Janice who was taking down the minutes. "Seconded by Tom Deakin." John then cleared his throat, more for effect than need. "I think we can all say that the 'Meet the pro night' was a success. Certainly everyone I've spoken to enjoyed themselves."

Janice raised her hand, and then interrupted. "Mr Chairman!" she shouted. "So the concept of somebody enjoying themselves is based on whether they are paralytic or not is it? Well I think it's a disgrace, there were people being ill all over the place. And you," she pointed at Tom, "obviously didn't get involved in the clean up. It was disgusting, sick everywhere, place stank to high heaven. You can still smell it now. We had to use over a gallon of bleach."

"And now it stinks like a public lav," he observed dryly.

"Ok, let's get back to business," John intervened. He turned and beckoned at the treasurer. Well, it was also a fund-raising night. How did we do Fred?"

Fred, a studious plain speaker whose clean-cut appearance reflected the way he did the accounts said, "Well, Mr. Chairman, I've worked it all out and taking into account into the cost of cleaning sundries purchased the following day, the event made two hundred and fifteen pounds."

"Not bad eh," said Arthur positively.

Fred then interjected in his official, dour manner, and they instinctively knew it would be bad news. "Mr. Chairman, can I put this into perspective. We said we would pay Benjamin six grand, i.e. three hundred a week. We have paid him one week's pay. We owe him two, and we have fifty six pounds in the bank"

One by one, as the dire circumstances registered, mouths fell open.

"On a happy note, beer's ok," said Tom, consuming it with his usual relish.

"Mr. Chairman" continued Fred, "the logic of the situation is that we need a 'Meet the Pro' night each week, just to break even," he advised more in jest than fact.

Everyone apart from Janice looked up and smiled. Instead she issued a warning.

"If you think I'm cleaning up the mess every Sunday you must be bloody mad, and that's swearing."

The meeting over, Tom and Arthur were in discussion, leaning against the bar sampling the brewery's latest offering. "We need a do that won't cause a lot of noise, doesn't need a crowd and that a select few would be willing to pay good money for." In unison they whispered, "A strip night," followed by a dirty laugh.

Joe Lagg, Start Of A Bad Day

The sun was streaming through the window of J Lagg, Estate Agents. Joe was in a good mood as he stuck bogus sold stickers onto details of bogus houses. "Got to get the housing market moving somehow, create a bit of panic. A legitimate tactic," he told himself.

Julia, his secretary, was giving him a piece of her mind. "I'm quite fond of the sun myself. Tenerife, Ibiza, Malaga, anywhere really, but not when it's glaring onto the sodding computer screen. If there are any errors it's not down to me, daft idea, everyone who walks past gawps at me, gives me the creeps."

"We've got to give the high tech impression, it's what the punter wants, see their name on a print out, they go for it," he reassured in a false 'Jack-the-lad' accent.

"Still a crap idea," she pressed.

The futility of the argument got the better of him so he retired to the back office and the quick crossword. A couple of easy clues focused his attention, so he didn't hear the door open as Julia poked her head through. Seeing he was miles away, she raised her voice above the normal volume required for communicating with someone not more than six feet away.

"Sorry to disturb your important meeting but there's a Mrs. Perkins to see you," she yelled.

The freshly-made coffee he held in his hand spilled as he jumped and the newspaper funnelled the drink quite neatly onto his lap. "No, no!" he shouted as the hot liquid seeped through to his underwear and touched a very delicate area.

"Mission accomplished," thought Julia. "You can go through now," she advised Susan cheerily.

Susan put a puzzled expression on her face. "Are you sure he's ready?" she queried.

"Oh yes," she replied. "He's a high-tech professional," she added as she went back to her seat in the window.

Susan entered the office without further ado to be confronted by Joseph standing with legs apart and pulling at the front of his fly. Taking advantage of his dilemma she did not hesitate. "Always wet yourself when you hear my name do you, well you'll do much worse if things don't begin to move."

He ushered her to a seat whilst continuing to hold out the front of his trousers. "Mrs. Perkins, please sit down, lets discuss this, peaceable like."

"So, what have you done then?" she asked trying to maintain the aggression.

Sitting back in his chair and still dabbing his trousers with a tissue he explained. "Well, err, nothing, you see we have to be patient, we're playing a waiting game."

Susan leapt in again. "So how long are we going to be patient for then, a week, a fortnight?"

Joseph looked at the cardboard pyramid shaped calendar on his desk. "By my calculations, another seventeen weeks."

"Curious amount of time?" she queried.

Julia, who had been hesitating at the door with a tray of coffee, offered, as Joseph put it later, an unhelpful input. "Longer, if we get through the next round," she said cryptically and left.

Still puzzled, Susan posed, "What does she mean?"

"Nothing, just ignore her, got it on her today, look if all goes according to plan it will be just seventeen weeks."

They finished the coffee in silence. Joseph looked through the window. It had clouded over and had started to rain. "At least she'll be able to see the bloody screen," he muttered.

Later, Same Day, The Perkins' House

Geoffrey was analysing the deadlines and target figures issued by his new boss. "I'll never achieve these, not in the time that's left," he said desperately.

Hearing his plight from the kitchen and working on the premise that a trouble shared is a trouble doubled, Susan offered only a modicum of support. "Achieve what, in what time?" she enquired with little interest in her voice.

Geoffrey, amid panic, tried to explain. "He wants me to sell three barrels of each beer to each cricket club in the Nethersdale League by the end of the season."

"That must be ages off, you can do that," she said supportively not knowing if he could or not.

Geoffrey continued, his voice sounding strained, "Seventeen weeks is all that's left, and most have already got fixed up with ale!" Beads of sweat formed on his brow. He waited for a reply that would at least go some way to solve the problem.

Susan though, had switched off to him the moment he mentioned the time scale. "Coincidence, never," she whispered. She put her head round the door, "What's seventeen weeks?"

"You're not listening!" shouted Geoffrey as the frustration got the better of him. "It's all that's left of the cricket season, except for them that gets through to the next round."

Susan went back to the ironing, "What are you up to Mr Lagg?"

Roland Bullock, The Story So Far

As boss of Bullock Units Ltd, Roland allowed himself a few luxuries. A new Jaguar, membership of the local but prestigious Premier Golf Club, even what was laughingly called a 'private box' at Hallifield Football Club. "For entertaining friends and business colleagues," he told the grounds man, who, for the purposes of conducting the transaction, had acquired the title of Director of Corporate Accommodation.

As he signed the cheque for another season, the chap replied in a manner totally unimpressed by Roland's bravado, "Whatever thy wants lad."

Roland looked round at the cold, stark, whitewashed walls that bore the names of sponsors. "It's always cold here," he said, then added, "Concrete, bricks, whitewash, and it stinks of liniment."

"You don't have to come here," replied the man replacing his tweed jacket for a brown smock.

"You're right, I don't." Roland had few friends, and even fewer business colleagues, so the box remained empty most of the time. These extravagances or 'Rightful perks of the job' as he put it, devoured his money. "It's ok, because it's the company's money, tax deductible," he would try and convince himself when the invoices needed signing. Fact was though that he couldn't play golf very well, and he wasn't that interested in football. He would show some excitement when he sank a put or the home team scored, but most of the time he would switch off and wonder what they saw in it, and why the hell he was there in the first place. Cruising round in his new car was all right but he didn't go anywhere other than to work and back. It was so smooth and quiet that he felt he was in a sterile steel box, cut off from other people, their lives, their interests, their fun, so the novelty of that soon wore off too. He was lonely and he knew it. Sometimes he would sit behind the wheel at traffic lights and shout, "I am so pissed off, is this what it's all about, just what the hell am I doing with my life?" If his tormented speech was meant as a cry for help, it failed, for not a word was heard from inside his sound-proof car.

He had acquaintances, he called them friends. They were only around during the football season or up for a free game of golf at his club, other than that he couldn't think of a single person he could relate to or confide in. "Is it me or them or what?" he would contemplate when feeling low.

He hated his childhood, all his dad's fault, even though he rarely saw him, too busy running his sodding mill, "His dirty horrible stinking mill."

"All this will be yours one day," his dad would promise, but he didn't want it then and he wanted it even less now.

He christened it, "The millstone around my frigging neck."

The other blight on his upbringing was his education. Worried about Roland's "Lack of nowse," as he put it, his dad sent him to a public school in order to, "Waken him up a bit."

Roland hated that too. He noticed it almost right away, for some reason he didn't fit in or get on with the other boys, it upset him terribly. "Why is it always me the jokes are played on?" he wondered.

He tried to lose his broad accent in an effort to fit in. It appeared to work for a while but after one tutor, a Mr Smythe, who had a pronounced speech impediment referred to him as "Master Bollock," the ribbing returned.

The other boys thought it hilarious to doodle sketches of a single hairy testicle across his work. So he would lie in his dormitory sobbing quietly so he could not be heard, with thoughts of escape running through his mind, but where to? He hated school and he hated home.

Roland didn't have much luck with the cricket either. His dad, who effectively owned the club, pulled a few strings to get him a place in the side, but after only three games of being totally out-classed and humiliated, he gave up. Unfortunately when the word got out how he achieved selection in the first place, his credibility sank to an all-time low. From then on he stayed away from the club and the deep-seated desire to get even with all concerned increased and intensified.

"My time will come," he would mutter when he recalled the treatment meted out to him by the players. Now and then he would drift, working out methods of retribution, it didn't take much, just a pause in the traffic, and not for the first time the blaring horn of a vehicle would bring him back to the present day.

"Ok, ok you bastard!" he shouted as he pulled away from the lights that had been green for what the lorry driver thought was a lifetime. "But this isn't a day for being hacked off," he reminded himself as he screeched into the courtyard of Bullock Units Limited. We've got ass to kick."

After the collapse of the cotton trade, plain Alfred Bullock as he was then, snapped up the mill for a song and immediately sold all the cotton machinery to other countries, which then made garments and exported them back to this country at a profit. Some embittered members of the community suggested that it was these 'dealings', or more likely the greasing of palms, that earned him the knighthood. He also, without any compassion, sold the gleaming original steam engine for scrap. It was a tragic day for the workers when they witnessed the destruction of their means of a livelihood.

Insult was added to injury twelve months later when he demolished all but the ground and first floor. "Be easier to manage," he reasoned.

There was no room for sentiment in the 'Alfred Bullock plan'. What could be sold as useful went out in one piece, what no longer had a part to play was broken up and sold as scrap. This not only applied to the mill engine, but masonry, well-oiled hardwood floorboards, everything. Until all that was left were the two floors. These were then converted into self-contained workshops and rented out to tenants on a yearly basis.

Roland enjoyed his position as landlord. He breezed into the office that hadn't been decorated since his father left. "Crap," he would comment every time he passed the false oak panelled walls that wobbled if pressed. "Christ knows why it's called beauty board," he asked himself for the hundredth time.

He sat in the big PVC swivel chair that made fart noises every time he moved, then leaned forward and rested his arms on the grand, well-used desk rescued from the mill manager's office. It was among only a few items to survive the ransacking occasion when Sir Alf bought the mill. Many a time he would question his father's taste of mixing classic grandeur with modern trash. This was highlighted by the so-called executive toys that were strategically placed for effect on the mahogany topped desk. He had thought about junking the lot, but on miserable days the chair had become a source of amusement. He had been known to laugh like a drain during discussions with a prospective tenant, when the noise would erupt at a poignant moment. He would collapse into a fit of laughter till the tears rolled down his face. Roland's dilemma was that the retention of the chair would look ridiculous in the presence of modern office furniture, and so rather than lose his object of fun, he persevered with the sixties facilities.

He sat in the chair with his hands gripping the edge of the PVC padded desk and announced in a booming voice to the walls. "But today we have some rental contracts to re-negotiate, no time for sentimentality, serious business to attend to. Marion, bring in the renewals file."

Marion, his long-suffering middle-aged secretary, raised her eyes to the ceiling. She only worked mornings just to get herself out of the house. She could easily walk away, but it paid for the niceties in life and all she really had to do, was put up with Roland. "What happened to 'please' and 'thank you', you ignorant little shite," she complained in a voice just low enough not to be heard.

One Such Tenant

Thomas Reagan, an electrical engineer, who rented a unit from Roland, was about to have his day turned upside-down.

"Yes, hello, what can I do you for?"

He spoke into the telephone that was also a FAX, a copier, a cassette player, a radio and an answer-phone. He liked to portray an image of modernity, of only using the latest up-to-the-minute equipment, but, as he recently experienced, high-tech gadgetry can have a down side. On the day that one of the resident rat population, in what must have been a serious depression, decided to commit suicide by chewing through the mains cable, it not only sentenced Thomas to a day of zero communication with the outside world, but also total silence in his workshop, and, as he described it later to his wife.

"Like being in solitary bloody confinement, with only the stench of burnt rat for company."

"Can I help you!" he bellowed down the phone, still not entirely convinced it was fixed.

On the other end of the line, Sir Alf thinking the man must be deaf replied at the same volume.

"Well I hope so, that's why I've rung!"

Sir Alf, not realising he was actually speaking to someone who rented a unit from him paused.

Thomas paused as well, and then shook the phone.

"Hello, you still there!" he shouted.

"Jesus!" cried Sir Alf as he held the phone away to prevent his eardrums bursting. He carefully put the receiver to his ear, and then decided to get in quick.

"I want this chair upgrading, it's too slow, can't catch her, costing a fortune," he said rapidly. Then as his words registered that he had gone too far, he backtracked.

"I just need it up-grading."

"You've got the wrong number, it's a joiner you need."

"No, no, an electrician," he replied realising the confusion he was causing.

"It's a wheelchair, an electric wheelchair, I want it up-grading, you know, faster, quicker and slicker and I want it to go over rough ground and for longer on a full charge," he explained.

"Hang on, hang on, and let me get this straight. You want me to make an electric wheel chair do all those things?"

"Are you, or are you not an electrical engineer?" he said impatiently.

"Well err, yes, it's just that it's a strange request that's all," Thomas added quickly, not wanting to throw business away. "Never had this type of request before, it's best if I come and see the problem," he suggested.

"If you're an electrical engineer there is no problem," responded Sir Alf.

"Still it's best if I see the, err, chair. What's the address?"

Sir Alf spelt out the address and gave him directions.

"Fine Mr Bullock, big house, top of the hill, no problem. When are you in then?" he asked innocently.

"I'm here all the bloody time, that's what it's all about," said Sir Alf snapping, and then wishing he hadn't.

"I'll just tidy up, then I'll set off."

The pleasantries over, they both hung up.

"Bullock, big house, top o'thill, that rings a small bell" he mused. He was just about to set off when Roland approached carrying a buff coloured envelope.

"Ah Mr Reagan, glad I caught you, how's business?" he patronised.

"Fine, what do you want?" he answered abruptly.

"It's now twelve months since you started here, and it's time we discussed the rental arrangement for the next period."

Thomas took the envelope and opened it. "Some discussion, you robbing bastard!" he remarked on seeing the contents.

"Now, now Mr Reagan let's keep things civil."

"It's gone up twenty percent, are you trying to ruin me?" he said, raising his voice.

"You just said business was fine, and if you recall, the first twelve months is always at a reduced rate to allow you to, settle in," he explained in a soft, false, caring way.

Thomas glared at him. "I seem to remember the word negotiation being used last year. This is bloody exploitation. You let me get set-up then dump me with this? Well, you can stuff your contract up your arse. Call again when you want to properly discuss terms," and he threw the envelope and its contents on the floor.

As he drove to Sir Alf's house his mind was full of devious plots of how to murder and then dispose of Roland Bullock. "Murder's easy, but how do you buy twenty gallons of hydrochloric acid and not get noticed?" He pondered this dilemma as he knocked on the front door.

"Mr Reagan," said Sir Alf, responding to the heavy-duty knock.

Thomas nodded.

Sir Alf observed the silence and sour expression. "You ok?" he inquired.

"Sorry, it's that bastard at Bullock Units, excuse the French," he said warming to Sir Alf's' concern. "He's just gone and put..." his complaint tailed of as the penny dropped. "Sorry Mr Bullock, only just realised, used to be your place," he added reddening with embarrassment.

"Still is my place, no need to be sorry, you're probably right. He is turning out to be a bit of a bugger."

Sir Alf looked at the floor. Now it was his turn to be embarrassed.

"Not a nice thing to say about your only son is it, but call a spade a spade."

He paused as they made their way into the kitchen, then he looked up and smiled at Thomas as a scheme developed in his head.

"But we might be in a position to do each other a bit of good."

Thomas looked at him sideways. "Oh?" he said cautiously.

"How about if I sort out your rent and you sort out my chair...deal?"

Sir Alf waited as Thomas ruminated over the proposal. "Deal," he replied, holding his hand across the kitchen table and smiling for the first time that day.

The Bullock's Kitchen, Suspicions Raised

Flora had never had it so good, pay off her visa, buy smart designer clothes and enough left for a hair-do. It had not gone totally unnoticed though.

Miriam Bullock was eyeing her up in the kitchen while Flora was watching the toast.

"Bit posh for doing housework in aren't they?" said Miriam in a sarcastic manner.

Flora turned, "I don't know what you mean."

"You know what I mean, your outfit, bit posh isn't it?"

"If you say so Mrs Bullock," said Flora urging the toast to brown in order to escape the inquisition.

"It was you I saw shopping in 'AEROS' the other day?" probed Miriam.

"Might have been, but I was only looking," added Flora, giving nothing away.

"You look like you're after something, or someone," she said bluntly.

"Nothing to do with you, what I do," she hissed, then sniffed the air and strutted into the breakfast room with the rack of toast.

Miriam followed, and then Flora retreated back to the kitchen.

"She's on the make, she's after our Roland."

Roland and Sir Alf looked up from their papers, and then in disbelief, looked back down again, but when Flora came back in again with the coffee, Roland took more notice. He looked her up and down then, as their eyes met, he smiled and winked. Flora in reply pulled out her tongue.

"I don't think so Mum," he said.

"Well who else could it be?" said Miriam.

Sir Alf kept his head in his paper and pretended not to notice. Recently in the pursuance of her job as housemaid, and, as the hidden participant in the game of hide and seek, Flora had discovered many unused rooms in the Bullock house. This mercenary quest was to avoid using the same hiding place twice and thus, keeping the resultant cash flowing. However, deep down inside she also held the view that she was being a bit hard, and so when she discovered a neat little bedroom that looked as though it hadn't seen daylight for years, she realised how she could repay him for all his generosity.

A Sunny Saturday Afternoon

Susan peered through the living room window. She glowered at the mesh fence that had become the iron bars to her prison.

"You mustn't play in the front garden," she said wagging a finger at Alison. "It's very dangerous. Those silly men could easily kill us, if we so much as set foot outside our own door."

Susan had become aware that her voice was beginning to sound a little cracked and paranoid. She clasped her hands to the sides of her head and looked down at her daughter.

"Can we play at the back?" Alison asked calmly.

"Err, yes, of course. Good idea," stuttered Susan, trying to regain her composure.

They held hands and were about to test this plan of playing in the back garden, when they heard a loud noise, followed by a huge cheer. It was the sound of a ball hitting the mesh window guard and the subsequent applause for a six hit by Benjamin.

He acknowledged the crowd's appreciation. But, as was explained to him at the start of the season, there was a downside to lofting balls straight down the pitch. It had become an unwritten rule at the cricket club that if you knocked the ball into the gardens opposite, it was up to you to go and get it.

Meanwhile in the Perkins's kitchen, Susan and Alison were frozen to the spot.

"You stay there," Susan whispered loudly, pointing underneath the kitchen table. She crept on all fours into the lounge.

"No damage so far," she reassured Alison, pretending she was still in control.

She peered out of the window and she still could not see any signs of a disturbance. Becoming braver, she crept into the vestibule and opened the front door a little. What happened next was too much for her.

Just about the time she had opened the door, Benjamin was about to press the doorbell. The sight of a huge black hand coming straight for her had taken her breath away.

Moments later, Benjamin was trying to explain to Susan the reasons for having to retrieve the ball, but with little success.

"You see Mrs, we gets awful grief from next-door, so no one wants to fetch it."

"How did I get here?" she asked, suddenly realising she was lying on her own settee.

"No problem Mrs, I just picked you up, seemed the thing to do."

"Yes, yes, of course," she said, looking up at the man who was having to bend his head to avoid touching the light fitting.

Susan thought she could deal with most situations, but she was shocked to find she could not take her eyes off the very prominent bulge in the front of his trousers. She had to fight back the intense urge to touch it.

"Mrs, is you all right, cos I gotta go?. I'll call back later to see if yuse ok."

Susan turned to see faces at the window. The other fielders had arrived to see what was causing the delay.

"Oh!" she yelped.

She was confused, hot and shaking. As he crossed the threshold of the front door, she was surprised to hear herself calling:

"Benjamin when did you say you were coming?"

As they trotted across the field, the other players mimicked her.

"When are you coming? When are you coming?" they laughed out loud.

Benjamin grinned.

"Never fails. Soon as they see my huge box, they're hooked."

Susan stared at the ceiling, which appeared to be spinning.

"Be out in a minute!" she called to Alison who was playing outside.

Susan felt strange. She was exhausted, tingling all over. Although it wasn't a particularly hot day, she was sweating.

Later in the day, she confided this to one of the women she had got friendly with on the school run. She stared into her coffee for inspiration, trying to make sense of it all.

"It was just as though I'd had, you know, dealings with him," she explained cryptically, then coloured up with embarrassment.

"Well if that happens just by looking, imagine what the real thing could do for you," said her friend, finishing the comment with a dirty laugh.

But Susan was way ahead of her.

A Strip Night Is Suggested

"It's not a strip night. It's a men only night with an exotic dancer," Tom Deakin said unconvincingly.

He was struggling to convince Arthur Padstow and John Appleby that this would be a good idea for raising funds.

"Janice will frigging kill us if she finds out. And how do we explain where the money comes from? Fred won't believe it's an anonymous donation. I tell you, it's fraught with problems," said John, nervously.

"Fred's in on it," smiled Tom smugly.

"You're joking! That prude?"

"He might be a prude, but he likes a gamble. He said it's ages since he had a game of brag. And I've told him about the disco dancer."

"Disco dancer? Oh my god, this is getting worse," said Arthur rubbing the perspiration from his forehead. "He will go frigging mad when he finds out."

"Well, he won't find out, will he ~ leastways not until it's too late. Then we'll say they sent the wrong woman. Look, we have to have him in on this to shuffle the money. Janice will be none the wiser."

"Let me get this straight," said Arthur. "You've told Fred that on the night we're having a game of dominoes, there's this woman coming round to dance for us. Jesus, he will hit the frigging roof when he finds out."

"I can't believe he's fallen for it," said John shaking his head. Then, with a dirty leer, he enquired: "Where did you get this woman from anyway?"

"Mate of mine put me onto this agency. Only fifty quid."

"You get what you pay for, you know. Must be a scrubber."

The beer had loosened their inhibitions and reservations. So with tears of laughter rolling down his face, Tom added the final insult:

"Well if she's not up to it, she can help Janice clean out the club."

Hide and Seek

Sir Alf had just had his best chase yet. He managed to get close to Flora's location, but his time ran out and those few seconds had cost him the statutory twenty-five pounds. 'Got to sort this out,' he thought. He handed over the cash whilst forcing a smile.

"Flora, I don't know where you hide these days. I'm losing track of the places to look."

It was true. Flora had found rooms that according to the level of dust, appeared never to have been entered since they moved in.

"If you think I'm giving my secrets away..." she laughed.

In a split second, she reflected on the quandary of having a lucrative source of income, but at the same time feeling rotten about not giving anything in return.

She kissed him on the forehead, then immediately wiped the lipstick away with the rag she used on the banister rail.

"Got to crack on," she said cheekily.

She wandered up the stairs, giving the rail an extra rub as she went.

'Got to get the odds more even,' he thought. He sneaked a look at Flora's legs as she skipped up the stairs. He sighed. Then, as she got out of earshot, he muttered: "Not only is it costing me a mint, but it's rousing sensations I thought were long dead... must ring the man about the chair."

He was hunting for the phone number, when the doorbell rang.

"I'll get it!" he bellowed.

He was wheeling himself to the door, when it rang again.

"Ok, ok!" he shouted impatiently, not knowing who was on the other side.

He opened the door to find John Appleby standing there. They looked at one another for what seemed ages. Then Sir Alf broke the deadlock:

"Good Jesus John, it's been a long time. Come in, come in." John followed, but didn't get a word in. "Nobody comes up here," Sir Alf said with blunt resignation, "Never see anyone from one day to the next."

They went into the kitchen.

"Hope you don't mind, but I can manage better in here. Coffee?"

"Fine," said John uttering his first word.

They sat at the large kitchen table.

"I'm sorry," said John. "I'd no idea you were..." His words tailed off as he struggled for a tactful phrase.

"Disabled."

"Well err, aye, not many know."

"Fell off this frigging ladder, three feet from the ground. Didn't break anything. Just went numb from the waist down. Damaged a nerve, they said at the hospital. Sommat to do with my spine. They said the feeling would come back. But it's been getting on two years now, and, well, sod all…"

At this point, he was cut short by Flora who pushed open the door. Having heard all she wanted to hear, she thought it pointless to earwig any more.

She curtsied, grinned, and in a mischievous voice asked:

"Will that be all, your lordship?"

Sir Alf was taken aback, but amused:

"Yes Flora, that will be all till tomorrow."

"I'll be off then."

She curtsied, turned, and grinned as she left.

"You're not entirely alone then?"

John was now aware that his friend's situation was not as dire as he made out.

"She's just the maid, housekeeper like. Goes round with the mop, nowt else," said Sir Alf, attempting, but failing to justify her presence.

"Now John, nice to see you. But I gather you've not come round here for the social, what can I do for you?"

John dropped his head.

"Well it's like this… we're not after charity or a donation… but up at the club, things are getting out of hand."

"Good Jesus, how can running a cricket club get out of hand?"

"Well we've had to respond to this ten year rule of yours," he said, raising his voice.

"Look, I know what you're thinking. I tried to get it stopped, but my lad had already sent out the letter. At present he runs the show, till I'm back on me feet. Not the best arrangement I'll grant you," he half-apologised, and then turned the argument round. "Point is though, what the hell's going on up there? The rule was devised so any tin pot club could handle it. You only have to win a cup or sommat once in ten years. Not a lot to ask is it?"

John rose to the defence of his colleagues, and as he did so, added grit to his voice.

"We put up with a lot of crap. We manage on minimum income and sod-all equipment. We put in loads of hours to keep the club fit for visitors. The players just play and piss off. Everyone thinks it looks after itself. Well it doesn't. We do it ~ the committee." He paused for breath then carried on. "We've overlooked this soddin' rule of yours, but if someone else thinks they can do a better job, then let 'em try." He stood up to leave.

"Hey, steady on. Sit down," Sir Alf responded, realising he had touched a nerve.

John calmed down. But, still disturbed, he went on:

"Your lad, he's mixed us a right bottle. Basically, we've no money. We exist hand to mouth each week. But to solve this problem, we've had to invest in this pro'. He's not cheap. Some money's coming in, but we need to pay some of his wages up-front. Do you follow? No money, no pro. No pro, no win. No win, no Cup… No Cup, no club. Simple"

Sir Alf scratched his head.

"No effing idea. How much are you short?"

"About two grand would tide us over." John hissed in through his teeth as he spoke.

Sir Alf fell back in his chair. "Hell… things have changed. Who've you got ~ Richie bleeding Benaud?"

"Benjamin Saxon's his name."

Sir Alf, slightly over-acting, looked at the ceiling:

"Jesus, have we none of our own who can do the business?"

"We would if we had, but we haven't," John replied pointedly.

"Well it's a sad state… I'll see you get your two grand. But it's only a loan, understand?"

John smiled. "Thanks Alf, you're a good un."

"Think I need sommat a bit stronger," said Sir Alf peering into his empty cup.

John, now smiling even more broadly, didn't need asking.

"You should get yourself to the club. We've got the best ale in town. Sheep's Head it's called."

As Sir Alf poured out the drinks, his mind was racing in other directions: 'Two grand here, mods to the chair, more cash for Flora. God's sake, best go see the man at Barclays…'

He looked up to see John looking at him expectantly:

"What was that?" he said. "Who's got a sheep's head?"

The Ram Inn

The refurbished and renamed Ram Inn now had a more relaxed atmosphere. Gone were the widescreen televisions on which the locals could watch sport. The old-fashioned jukebox had been replaced with mindless, continuous mood music.

"We're after a different type of clientele, more respectable and discerning... people with *taste,*" said the new barman, Ralph Adler. He emphasised the point with a simpering smile, as if the person he was addressing didn't fit the description.

"People with money you mean," chipped in a regular from the previous incarnation of the pub, clearly dissatisfied with the changes.

"Before you did it up, you could get a pint for less than a quid. I need a bleedin' mortgage for one now."

"Ah, but its real ale now. It's been passed as excellent. We're in the 'Better Beer Book'."

Ralph pointed to a certificate behind the bar.

"Passed by the management," interrupted an irate customer.

"Pissed by them more like," added another.

The confidence of the customers to barrack the new barman grew.

"Sheep's Head? More like Sheep *Dip*," shouted a man at the back.

The intensity rose.

"One pound effing fifty, for sheep's piss."

"What the hell's going on?"

It was the owner of the pub, Anthony Dawes. He had dashed in when he heard the racket.

"Nothing boss, just a bit of light hearted banter," Ralph replied with a wobble in his voice.

An anonymous heckler from the back added to Ralph's apparent lack of control.

"Banter, banter! You put up our beer up by forty pee, then dish out this gnat's piss."

Anthony stepped in: "Gentlemen, gentlemen... please." He gained their attention, and then attempted to offset the disturbance. "I'm sure you'll agree the place is much better now since the modernisation, but we have to recover the..."

"More convivial," interrupted Ralph.

"Keep out," snapped Anthony, still maintaining a grin.

"Price's gone up and the beer's crap," shouted a complainer from the back.

"Crap! Crap? I'll have you know, this ale is a prize winner."

He responded by grabbing the pump handle. He pulled the ale into a pint glass, but immediately became suspicious.

"What the...?" He was lost for words as he looked at the cloudy liquid in the glass. He sipped and gritted his teeth.

"Good Jesus," he remarked spitting it back in the glass. "It's off!"

He pulled another pint and sniffed it.

"This is well off"

Ralph began to colour up.

"You've been serving sour beer all day?"

Ralph nodded.

"Change the barrel then apologise to all these folk. Give them their money back out of the till, and buy them a round out of your own pocket."

Ralph nodded again. As he pulled the round, the pub echoed to the chant of: "Easy, easy, easy."

At the back of the lounge, a group of men were being entertained by the goings on: Roland, Joseph Lagg and the brothers Simon and Reginald of Jakeson & Jakeson Builders and Property Repairers Inc. They had arranged to meet earlier, but had been temporarily distracted by the commotion.

"So, what have you to report?" Roland asked impatiently.

"We've done as you asked. Been round to his old club and snooped round," replied Simon, demonstrating what he had done by a facial expression.

Roland rolled his eyes.

"Get on with it!" he barked.

"Seems he was well liked, particularly by the women. Fathered a couple of kids by all accounts. Difficult to prove, though no one would commit themselves."

Roland, with a confused expression, butted in.

"Excuse me! Difficult to prove? The guy's black isn't he?"

They looked at him as though was talking a foreign language. Realising this, he waved his hands in surrender.

"No, no, it doesn't matter now. You carry on."

Simon took a deep breath.

"It were amazing though. They all said same thing, Big Ben strikes on the hour, every hour... it all got a bit too much."

Roland's patience was wearing thin.

"Yes, yes. But is there anything we can make use of?"

"Not really. He's just a nice bloke. In fact, we've been to watch him. Can't half knock a ball. He won the game in the last over. Everyone were jumping up and down and screaming. Near the top of the league now."

Roland's anger boiled over.

"Great, just great! I send two men out to do a bit of undercover muckraking, and they turn out to be clowns having a jolly on my expenses. Well you'll have to do better than this. The idea was to find something we can use to scotch him. No muck, no pay."

"Funny you should mention that," said Reginald thoughtfully.

"What, muck?" snapped Roland, now raising his voice.

"No… scotch," he continued. "Seems he gets melancholy after a few whiskey's, then goes on benders for days. Been known to go missing all week. Don't turn up for matches, nothin'. All it takes is one glass to set him off. So they were all keen to keep him away from the top shelf."

Roland leaned back into his chair and his face changed to a wry smile.

"That's better," he oozed.

Simon went to the bar flashing Roland's crisp tenner like a trophy. The others remained in their seats deep in thought. As the beers were put in place, Roland leaned forward and whispered his proposal.

"So all we have to do is get someone to get close to him, become his buddy. Then one Friday, they buy him a few drinks ~ and bingo!"

They all looked at Joe.

"You can get stuffed if you think I'm doing your dirty work," he rapped.

"Look," Roland said softly, indicating that he really did want Joe to do his dirty work. "All you've got to do is get cosy with him. It's weeks away from any… dirty work."

"Not happy, not happy" protested Joe.

The brothers sniggered.

"It's got to be a vital game, one that the league or a cup depends on. That's where you two come in."

In unison, the smirk fell from the brothers' faces.

"Us?" they protested.

"It's up to you two to figure out which game is the clincher. It'll have to be a home game and played on a Saturday. With a bit of luck, we'll skittle him for the whole weekend. Two matches in one go."

"Just like the little tailor," chipped in Simon.

The others, bemused, stared at him blankly. Then Reginald, embarrassingly, offered an explanation.

"It were flies, and there were seven of them, you thick bastard."

"Don't call me a thick bastard," he shouted across the table.

"For God's sake sit down and keep quiet! This was supposed to be an inconspicuous meeting, not a friggin' bar room brawl," Roland hissed. "Now, you know what you have to do?"

They nodded in agreement.

"Just think of the holidays you can have after we pull this off. Now anyone want a Sheep's Head?"

Reginald looked at Simon: "I'm gonna have you outside..."

Roland wandered off to the bar, perplexed at how he had got mixed up with them and casually ordered:

"Three idiots please."

Saturday Morning, Ready To Go

Geoffrey put on his coat and grabbed his car keys. He was almost ready to set off on another mission, trying to get clubs to change their existing brewery to his. However, he paused and turned back up the hall. He sensed a change. Not being able to put his finger on it, he offered a simple but probing question:

"What have you got on today? Shopping?"

"Done that," said Susan.

"Did it yesterday," confirmed Alison.

"Going to see your Mum then?"

"No, not today."

Susan did not lift her eyes from the freezer box she was filling.

"Ah, going on a picnic?" he said confidently.

"Not exactly a picnic…"

"We're going to watch Benjamin," said his daughter.

"We're going to the cricket," Susan quickly interrupted. "Strange as it may seem, we've less chance of being hit by the ball if we're at the ground."

"Who's Benjamin?" asked Geoffrey.

"He's a big black man," giggled Alison.

"He's the professional at the cricket club," Susan added with authority.

"He's ever so strong. He carried Mummy from the doorway and put her on the settee, just like she was a baby," said Alison with mischief in her voice.

Geoffrey's face set in a glare.

"First I've heard of this, what's been going on?"

"Nothing's going on. It's a long story. I'll tell you later," she said, still staring into the bottom of the freezer box in order to avoid eye contact.

"Look, we must go or we'll miss the toss," she added trying to put a stop to the topic.

Geoffrey scowled.

"I'll get an explanation from you later, do you hear?"

His voice tailed off as he stomped down the hallway and slammed the door. Seconds later, the noise of a revving engine was heard.

"Now see what you've done, you've made Daddy all upset," Susan said, grinning as she screwed the top on the Thermos.

Sir Alf Ventures Out

The taxi approached the main street in Throttle centre. Here, a mix of large Victorian properties interspersed with modern concrete shops. Sir Alf stared out of the taxi window. Although it had not been that long since he visited the place, he could have sworn it had changed.

"Don't recognise any of these shops," he muttered to the back of the driver's head. The driver pulled up outside the bank.

"Just dump me here. I'll be all right."

"You sure?"

Sir Alf nodded impatiently. The driver rolled his eyes:

"Your funeral," he coughed, as he rummaged in the boot, then put the steel ramps to the pavement.

"Here, keep the change."

"Cheers," said the driver in a voice designed to indicate his disgust at the twenty pence tip. As the driver helped him out of the taxi, his face suddenly lit up.

"Knew I'd get it! You're Alfred Bullock, the mill owner."

Sir Alf looked at him.

"I used to be, look at me now. Want to swap?"

"Not a chance," he replied unkindly, as he helped him down the ramp.

Sir Alf looked up at the bank. It was a place he had visited many times before, albeit not for a couple of years. Before, he hadn't bothered about the large imposing doorway or the grand steps up to the entrance. As he sat in the chair, it all looked much taller than before. All of a sudden, he felt helpless. Although it wasn't a hot day, beads of sweat began to form on his forehead. His mind raced back to the meetings he had attended here, important meetings. He used to strut around in this place. The managers (and he'd seen a few) would fawn over him because he had wealth, and wealth meant power.

"And now I can't even get into the frigging place!" he shouted in despair.

A queue of people at the nearby bus stop turned and stared, but did not help. He felt embarrassed and angry.

Then a voice from behind spoke out: "Is it Mr Bullock?"

He looked up. At the top of the steps, a dark-suited young lady repeated the question.

"Mr Bullock, to see Mr Roscoe?"

He nodded.

She skipped down the steps and grabbed the wheelchair handles.

"The disabled entrance is round the corner," she said urging him on.

"I am not disabled," he advised sternly, "Just a temporary problem with me legs. I am quite capable of operating this chair on me own."

Seconds later, he gripped the sides of the wheels and stopped.

"Young lady," he said, but now in a softer voice tinged with remorse.

"Call me Linda," she replied.

"Linda, I'm sorry, it's just that I used to stride in here without a second's thought. But now it's a major operation."

She smiled.

"No problem, this way Mr Bullock."

Humbled, he thought, 'What a rotten bastard thing to do.'

Once inside, she pushed him towards a large oak panelled door, and gently knocked. Seconds later, the door opened.

"Sorry I'm late, I couldn't find the entrance," Sir Alf apologised.

"No problem at all. You're right about the ramp. Planners wouldn't let us put it at the front. They said it would ruin the façade," said Mr Roscoe.

Sir Alf looked round the bank manager's office. Gone was the leather chair and dark oak desk with inkstands. These had been replaced with soft furnishings, and a computer on the end of a semi-circular plastic topped unit.

"Curious that you should make an appointment today," he said casually, bringing Sir Alf back to the point of the visit.

"Oh, why's that?"

"We had your Roland in here only last week. Milk with your coffee?" he asked, as Linda rattled down the cups.

Sir Alf gripped the sides of his chair.

"Our Roland, what did he want?

Mr Roscoe looked at him sideways.

"Surely you know? The loan for the new development?"

"Loan? Loan! What do we want with a loan? Company's well off with all the income from the units," he said, beginning to get worked up.

There was a pause as Mr Roscoe rattled the keys of the computer, then stared at the screen. He leaned back in his chair, raised his eyebrows and pointed with an open palm to the screen.

"I'm afraid, at present, the income barely covers the outgoings. I'm sorry to say that between the two directors, Miriam and Roland, most off the income is spent."

Sir Alf went quiet. He took his time as he dunked a biscuit in his coffee. 'Keep calm, keep calm,' he told himself.

"Right Mr Roscoe. Yes, of course, the proposed new development. Still at the feasibility stage… anyway I could do with a few quid for my personal use. About five grand should cover it."

"No problem Mr Bullock, peanuts compared to four hundred and fifty thousand."

Sir Alf's cup wobbled on the saucer: "Four hundred and fifty…"

"Apparently, the scheme to redevelop the cricket ground will cost at least that. Of course if all the houses are sold above their target price, you should more than double your investment."

Sir Alf went cold. Not for a long while had he experienced so many emotions in such a short time.

"And can I advise you Mr Bullock, that for a man of your integrity, it isn't necessary to make an appointment to withdraw five thousand pounds. Just give the bank a ring and we'll have it ready for you. Is there anything else I can help you with?"

He shook his head, but not in reply to the question.

Moments later Sir Alf, plus bulging brown envelope in his inside pocket, found himself on the pavement outside.

"Be all right will you Mr Bullock?" said Linda.

She lowered her voice to avoid drawing unnecessary attention.

"I think so," he mouthed.

His mind still racing, he set off in the direction of Cargill & Sons Solicitors.

At home, he was used to having unhindered access when moving about. Ramps, widened doors and lifts had been installed so he could move around freely. But negotiating the pavements and crossing the roads was a new experience for him. There were people in the way, prams, dogs, lampposts, telephone boxes. Crossing the road became a life-threatening matter. He gasped as huge lorries passed within inches.

"The bastards aren't even slowing down," he muttered to himself at the kerb edge.

He looked up and down the street.

"Jesus," he said out loud as a huge van nearly wiped him out. He was just about to try again when he was rescued by a familiar voice.

"Need a lift?"

He turned to see the taxi driver leaning out of his cab window.

"If you don't mind," he said panting.

"Different world isn't it? My old man used to get so screwed up when he went out in his chair," said the driver, opening the cab door. "Where to?"

"Cargill & Sons Solicitors."

"Good job I came along," laughed the driver. "It's the other end of town. You'd have been ages."

Sir Alf took a deep breath:

"Got to sort this out… all of it."

He pondered his plight for a moment and a slight depression came over him. The driver, however, had his own opinion.

"You've got it easy," he announced. "Big house, plenty of helpers, cash."

Sir Alf's jaw fell open.

"My old man used to work in your mill before you had it!" said the driver, partially turning his head. "His insides got clogged up with the fluff till he hadn't the breath to walk. We pushed him for miles in his chair, trying to get some fresh air into him. Died about ten years ago."

Sir Alf was trying to think of something suitable to say. But they had already arrived at the solicitors, so he was saved from the quandary.

"Do you want me to wait?" asked the driver.

"Best not. No knowing how long I'll be," he replied choosing his words carefully. "But you can help me inside if you will."

Once inside, he found himself looking up at another high counter.

"Is Terry Cargill in?" he said.

"I'll just see if he can be disturbed," said the receptionist peering down at him and using an affected plummy voice.

"What is it about?" she further inquired, following orders from her boss to protect him from timewasters.

"That's between me and him," Sir Alf barked, leaving no doubt that it was a private matter.

Startled, she wondered if it was worth the pittance of a wage having to deal with this kind of confrontation. She sniffed the air, looked down her nose, turned and entered the door marked *Private*.

As the automatic door closed slowly, her voice, now having reverted back to her native accent, could just be heard:

"If you think I'm putting up with this crap all the time..."

Sir Alf smiled and wheeled himself over to the waiting area. He picked up a magazine. No sooner had he opened it, than a voice from the old days enveloped him:

"Alf, how are you? Sorry for... you know what I mean..." he was staring at the wheelchair. "Come in, for goodness sake. Agnes, make us a brew. It's one of my old mates."

Sir Alf was right not to keep the taxi driver waiting. The pleasantries, the tea and biscuits, and finally the reminiscences, all very easily took over an hour.

"What brings you here? Surely not just passing?" Terry said looking at the clock and realising the time.

"It's confidential. I need your help, but I also need your word it won't go any further."

Terry swung his chin from side to side as he straightened his tie, a mannerism that Sir Alf suddenly remembered.

"We go back a long way, you and me. If we can't help each other in a crisis, it's a poor do."

"Well it's our Roland. He's about as much idea as…"

"I'd heard whispers," butted in Terry.

"What whispers?"

"It's difficult to say. They're only rumours," edged Terry.

"Come on out with it!"

"Well, he's getting himself in a bit of a mess. Not to mention mixing with a few, how can we say, 'less than straight' individuals."

"For Christ's sake Terry, speak your mind."

"Here it is then, as much as I know. Apparently the books aren't balancing as they should… You know, the recession… it's hit a lot of folk hard, particularly the one-man bands who rent small units. You do know that half your units are empty?"

"No."

"So the income is halved. But he still has his new Jag's and posh living. From what I've heard, he's trying to borrow his way out of trouble. I tell you, if it goes pear-shaped he'll take you with him."

Sir Alf stared forwards but did not focus. His mind was racing back over the past twenty years of graft and deals to the point where he thought he was handing over a doddle of a job to his son. 'Take the rent, install a new tenant. Take the rent, install a new tenant. That's all he has to do. What could be simpler?' he thought, holding out his palms.

"All that time building it up and in less than three years he's made a balls of it."

"He doesn't keep you in touch then?" sympathised Terry.

"Not a word. Thought everything was going ok," winced Sir Alf.

"We thought you knew…"

"I've got to get back in control. Can you give us a hand?"

"I'll do what I can. But, well, we all thought you were a bit hasty handing it over like you did. Office boy to chairman! He won't be easy to shift."

"My fault really. I thought he could handle it. With my accident an' all, I weren't thinking straight."

Terry tried to cheer him up.

"I'll do some checking, I'm sure we can sort it out… Agnes can you call a cab?"

Sir Alf smiled: "Remember the one that fetched me?"

"Yes, Rally Cabs, I think it was," Agnes said.

"Any but that."

Susan and a Quandary

Susan was part way through the drudge of house cleaning. But on this particular day, she had her mind on other things. Things that kept getting in the way of her doing her usual, acceptable effort at keeping the house ready to be re-wrecked and re-soiled. She switched off the noisy vac' and sat on the edge of the bed. She pondered the recent few days and wondered how on earth life could get so complicated.

'One minute everything's honky dory. The next, all hell breaks loose. Here I am, so-called happily married: daughter healthy and normal; nice house albeit in the firing line of the cricket; husband with a reasonably secure job. So why ruin it all? Why risk all this for that?'

These thoughts went through her mind as she watched Benjamin going round and round the cricket pitch on the motor mower. He had agreed to complete this time-consuming task as the club was short of volunteers.

"All I have to do is sit here," he said.

Susan moved over to the window and pulled up the little padded chair that usually sat in front of the dresser. Elbows on the sill and head in hands, her mind kept raising questions.

"What is it? Infatuation, lust, desire? I don't fancy him like you fancied a boy at school. It's not love."

But whatever 'it' was, it made her uneasy, unable to relax. 'It' was always on her mind, 'It' bugged her.

"So what is it?" she shouted as her eyes followed the mower on its tighter and tighter route to the centre of the pitch. She loved Geoffrey, and they had sex whenever *she* wanted it. 'So,' she pondered, 'What's going to be different?'

This she didn't know. But one thing she did know was that as soon as she caught sight of Benjamin, her breathing rate increased, her legs went to jelly and she began to feel hot. In fact, she was sweating now. Having recently read self-help books entitled, 'How To Be Assertive', immediately followed by 'Feel the Fright and Do It Anyway', she felt it her duty to go and get whatever she desired. In her own words: "Hang the consequences." This phrase echoed back moments later when she thought about the sentences handed out to adulterous wives in the Far East. Sitting back on the edge of the bed, she took a deep breath.

"But that is there and this is here. And I'm not getting any younger."

So that was it. She had to know what it was that nearly poked her eye out when she came to her senses on the settee that fated Saturday afternoon. She stood up just in time catch a rear view of Benjamin as he drove the mower into the shed.

"You're only here once! And Benjamin is only here another fifteen weeks, so I'd better get my skates on."

As she made her way downstairs she began to plot.

"Mmm, got to get closer. Need an excuse, a reason for being there."

As she arrived in the kitchen, she added several words to the bottom of the shopping list. *Cricket rules. Ground maintenance. Running a committee.*

"That should do for starters."

The Go-Faster Wheelchair

Sir Alf was mulling over his new problems when the phone rang.
"Tom Reagan here... your chair, we've made it better. Don't half go. It's ready, can I bring it round?"
"Of course you can... I'm in all day," Sir Alf sighed. He put the phone down, but spoke as if there was still someone there. "Be glad of a distraction, take my mind off everything else."
It didn't seem long before the front door bell rang.
"You must have been phoning from the end of the drive."
"Why?... What do you mean?" came the bewildered reply.
Sir Alf began to realise that maybe it was his daydreaming that had caused the confusion.
"You'll have to excuse me, I'm having an off day."
"Nobody's perfect," Tom retorted in an unsympathetic huff.
Sir Alf threw out a lifeline:
"Let's start again. Would you like a coffee?"
"That'd be grand. I'll be getting it out of the van."
Sir Alf smiled and wheeled into the kitchen. Five minutes later, he returned balancing a tray of drinks. As soon as he saw the new chair, his bottom jaw appeared to have become separated from the rest of his mouth.
"Eeee... that looks...bloody excellent!" he said with obvious delight.
"I've done some extra mods."
"You've done what?" replied Sir Alf, whilst running his fingers near a vertical handle with a red top.
"Don't touch that!" Tom shouted. "It'll be off like a shot if you move that."
Sir Alf pulled back his arm as though he had received an electric shock.
"Are you sure this is going to be all right?" he winced.
"You'll get used to it. Now, about these mods, err... alterations," Tom said, trying to reduce the jargon. "First off, it's a lot, lot, faster. It's got four high-revving instant-response motors, four-wheel drive if you like. The power will come in smooth if you want, or all at once, because of this power actuator."
"Throttle," said Sir Alf.
"What?" replied Tom.
"Throttle, it's a bleeding throttle."
Tom ignored him, and carried on enthusiastically:
"The steering has an improved lock. We've got bigger, wider, tyres." At this point, he had to physically restrain himself from touching the wheels. "Lights, indicators and a horn. What do you think of the seat?"

He smiled squeezing the leather upholstery. "Got it out of an old Mini Cooper, complete with full race harness."

Sir Alf stared.

"Seem to remember fighter pilots had these during the War!"

Undeterred by Sir Alf's comment, Tom ploughed on.

"If you're going off-road, it's a good idea to have one of these," he pointed towards the cardboard box alongside the chair.

Sir Alf reached inside and removed a shiny red crash helmet.

"I checked with the police. They say it's not compulsory, just a good idea."

The expression on Sir Alf's face indicated that things were getting out of hand.

"Just wait till you try it! We've had endless fun testing it. Oh, just one thing…" he added. "The police did say that if you exceeded the speed limit, you'd be in a bit of bother. So go easy till you get used to it."

"Really?" Sir Alf replied, warming to the idea.

"Oh aye. We've not had it flat out ~ couldn't find a road long enough. These motors will rev up to nine thousand r.p.m. That's fifty odd miles an hour."

"Hell fire!" Sir Alf said, a hint of excitement creeping into his voice.

"Nethen, this clock tells you how much battery you've got left. As soon as you move, it starts ticking away. The faster you go, the faster the clock ticks, get it?"

Sir Alf stared at the gleaming paint and racing seat. Inside, he was aching to have a go.

"What do I owe you?"

"Four hundred and fifty quid for the parts," said Tom handing him an invoice.

"And the labour?" Sir Alf asked.

"Forget that, just sort out your lad."

Tom climbed into his van and wound down the window.

"Any problems, give us a bell. Oh, and don't forget the hat."

Sir Alf hadn't been this excited since… well, he couldn't remember when. Within minutes he had swapped chairs, adjusted the seat belt and although he didn't think it necessary, had put on the helmet just to see what it felt like. Hesitantly, he turned the key and gently pushed forward the lever. He heard the motors whine as the chair edged forward.

"Bloody hell," he muttered inside the helmet.

That afternoon he explored the whole grounds and beyond. He found places he had long forgotten about, and places within easy reach that he had never seen. As he located wooded glades and open views across the valley, Miriam's words came back to haunt him:

"Too busy looking after your soddin' mill…" 'Maybe if we'd gone on walks together, things would have been different?' he pondered.

Coming back up the drive, he looked at the clock. 'Loads of time left,' he thought. 'Let's see what it can do.'

He pushed the lever forward to its maximum. Gravel flew from behind each wheel, and his head was thrown back. As the wheels fought for traction, the chair veered from side to side. He had to fight the steering to keep it in the centre of the drive. Seconds later, he came to screeching halt as the hydraulic disc brakes locked up each wheel. He flicked up the visor, excitement coursing through him. He sat for a moment then undid the strap and lifted off the helmet. He didn't know whether to laugh or cry. His heart pounded so loud he could hear it. He looked down and saw his hands trembling.

"Get a grip," he urged himself.

He always considered himself to be in control. Even after the accident, visitors were impressed that he took the news of his impending confinement 'like a man'. His present condition was, he considered, totally out of character. Tears were not in his make up, but he couldn't control himself. He had a lump in his throat and his eyes watered. He took out his hanky, and with a shaky hand, blew his nose.

'Can't be seen like this,' he chided himself, even though the possibility of anyone calling was remote. After a minute or so, he had calmed down. He looked at the clock, and then wiped it with his hanky.

'Another four hours left. I'll just have a brew, and then I'll test it again.'

Dusk

As the light faded, Geoffrey Perkins checked all the doors on his car. It wasn't the first time. He had been out there only an hour before, pulling at the handles to see if they were locked. He blamed this apparent loss of memory on a continuous alcohol intake.

"As a salesperson, I'm expected to demonstrate just how good my product is, a cross I must honourably bear in order to feed my wife and child," he rambled as he re-entered the kitchen.

"What are you wittering about?" asked Susan at the sink.

"More meetings than sodding NATO," he replied.

"Where?" she said, turning and dripping water on the floor.

"Over there, men in suits, entering the club."

He pointed out of the window towards the clubhouse.

Susan's inquisitive nature got the better of her. She put on her shoes and went down the driveway. Geoffrey followed her.

"See!" he said, as a steady stream of well-dressed men knocked on the door, surreptitiously looked around, and then quickly entered.

"Sommat going on up there. And it's not bingo."

"Your suspicious mind will get you in trouble one of these days," Susan mused.

She returned to the kitchen, and immersed her hands in what was now cold dishwater.

Miriam Escapes To Be Pampered

Miriam was relaxing at her favourite health club. She was on the first day of a long weekend break. Having just had a sauna, she was in the cooling off area. She was reclining on a wicker lounger wearing only a white towelling robe. She watched the other women dipping into the plunge bath and then going back to the sauna. To her amazement, some didn't bother with robes. 'Your body's got to be perfect to do that, and some clearly aren't,' she thought, as a middle-aged lady who obviously couldn't have cared less, wobbled by.

She closed her eyes to the view and tried to relax. But things, personal things, were on her mind. 'Plenty of money, no need to work. I should be ecstatic. So why aren't I?' She couldn't decide whether life was treating her badly or not. True, she was well off, but it hadn't gone as planned.

Her beginnings were quite humble and as a child she always wondered what it would be like to be rich. It seemed curious now, but the only jobs open to her when she was about to leave school were in the mill. And by the time she did leave, they had shut it. Instead, she ended up serving dinners at the local chip shop.

Unaware of his intentions, she served plain Alf Bullock for months before he got up the courage to ask her out. She had always dreamt of a whirlwind romance, but had to settle for being courted amidst the smell of hot fat and vinegar. Everyone thought she was so lucky being chosen by the owner of the mill.

In those days, life was a dream ~ from chip shop waitress to boss's girlfriend in one fell swoop. Big cars became the norm as did holidays down south.

But after the wedding, reality dawned and the novelty began to wear a bit thin. She thought that the arrival of Roland would provide her with the purpose in life she so dearly needed. It did for the first couple of years, until his father got the big idea that Roland should go away for his education. So, at the tender age of four, Roland was dragged away from his mother's embrace and packed off to prep' school. With him went Miriam's motherhood and enthusiasm. For the first term that Roland was away, she became depressed. She couldn't understand why her husband had insisted on sending the boy away, when clearly she needed him with her. From that point, cracks began to appear in their marriage. Now, as she looked back, she realised she never really loved him in the first place. It was his money and lifestyle she loved, but now she hated it.

The final straw came as she held out her arms to welcome the return of her son after only one term at boarding school. He had changed. His accent had gone all posh and he continually criticised her for "talking common". Mummy's boy had become a brat.

Whilst Roland was away at school and Alf was working, Miriam spent a lot of time on her own in the house. It was after yet another idle day, flicking through the magazines designed for women with time on their hands that she discovered what she thought would be an interest. This not only would help her get over the disappointment at home, but also maybe give her a much needed direction. She decided it was time to smarten the place up. 'Give me an excuse to invite folk over, have some parties,' she dreamed.

So she got interior designers in and had the place totally re-decorated: flock wallpaper, fancy coving, brash curtains, dado rails, swags and tails. "The business," as she put it. Sir Alf, with his usual disapproval, commented: "Put me out of bleeding business, the cost of all this."

To a degree, it worked. They had parties. But they were not the type of social gatherings she had envisaged, more friends coming for a nosy at the décor. The majority thought it brassy and usually ended up drifting to the pub.

Since the accident, and consequently the destruction of all her efforts to make the house fit for publication in 'Up North Life', she had lost all interest in the house. The thoughts of what he had wrecked in her absence made her reluctant to return home. So the role of wife and mother had become a sham, a token gesture. Just going through the motions.

She even went through the night class routine, thinking she would latch on to something arty or creative. But nothing grabbed her. The nearest she came to it was aromatherapy. She really enjoyed it till she was asked to give a massage to a person she described as "wrinkly," and it put her off so much she didn't return.

She was caught in a quandary. She had mulled it over time and time again. 'I need a purpose and an objective. But short-term, I need the money to take my mind off it all. But to keep the cash flowing, I have to be part of the Bullock family. Jesus what a mess, there has to be an answer.' The thoughts ran riot in her head. She had considered getting a divorce, even got to the front door of the solicitors, and then walked away. Just the thought of all the upheaval was enough to put her off, and then being presented with a lump sum. 'Just like being made redundant, probably blow it all in one go.' The record went round and round. 'No purpose, not happy, but plenty of cash, no purpose, not happy, but plenty of cash, no…'

A soft male voice interrupted her thoughts, releasing her from her torment:

"Time for the next stage Mrs Bullock. Are you ready?"

She opened her eyes and stared straight at the source of the request, a squeaky-clean young man with a beaming smile.

"You're dead right, I am love," she replied.

Mid Season Meeting

"Can I welcome you all to the fifth meeting of the season. I'd like to offer a particularly warm welcome to a new member, Mrs Susan Perkins. Good to have you on board. We're always grateful for an extra pair of hands."

Susan exchanged courteous glances with the other members.

"We've met before though, haven't we?" chipped in Tom Deakin. "You came to the karaoke night with your Geoffrey. He's the one who supplied the ale that night."

The others nodded, apart from Janice who just gritted her teeth.

"I couldn't stop long ~ baby sitter problems ~ but I heard it was a success," Susan enthused.

"Depends on how you rate success," Janice spat. "If you rate it on how much cleaning up you have to do afterwards, it were a roaring success. I can only say it's the last time I man the mop bucket. It were days before I stopped heaving and the smell..." To emphasise the point, she screwed up her face as though she had just bitten a lemon.

"Thank you for that personal revelation Janice, but we must move on," interjected John.

Wanting to put an end to the subject, Susan completed her prepared acceptance speech:

"Thank you for the warm welcome. I look forward to assisting the committee members in their endeavour to ensure the survival of the club."

Silently, she added what she really meant to say: 'and the opportunity of engaging in a bit of self-indulgence.'

John Appleby went on:

"That reminds me, I've had a letter from the brewery congratulating us on the condition of our pumps etc. They say that if we need any help, we..."

"Point of order Mr Chairman," said Susan interrupting him.

He looked over his glasses: "Yes?"

"Surely this item comes under the section of correspondence during the secretary's report?"

"Yes, but I thought it was relevant," said John taken aback.

"It might be relevant, but it's definitely correspondence," smirked Janice.

John looked at the others for support. They shrugged their shoulders.

"She's right," added Tom mischievously.

"Well I think it's nit-picking, supposed to be a friendly, social type of committee."

John, having taken umbrage, straightened his tie and then his glasses. He cleared his throat and added: "Anybody else wants to do this pigging job, they're welcome."

Janice, who didn't get that many opportunities to stick the knife in, continued: "It's not that we don't want you to continue. It's just that if job's worth doing, it's worth doing right..." She looked down at her lap to hide her smile, but failed.

"Can I move progress Mr Chairman, else I'm going to bugger off home," interrupted Fred in a much louder voice than usual.

"Hear, hear," added Tom, not wanting to be left out.

"Very well, can we have the secretary's report please," to which John sat down in a huff.

Arthur Padstow trudged his way through his list of items, until he reached an issue that fell right into Susan's lap.

"We're about a third of the way through the season. We could do with a quick appraisal of what we need to get us through the next third, a simple inventory. We're all right in the kitchen, that takes care of itself. It's the other bits and bobs ~ cleaning, toiletries ~ and to make sure we've got enough stuff in the shed."

"You mean whitening, loam, grass seed and petrol for the mower," Susan said authoritatively.

The others were shocked into silence.

"Yes, well err, aye, that sort of stuff," stuttered Arthur.

"No problem," said Susan.

"Just make a list, I'll do the rest. I don't mind, so long as you don't want it right away. I can pop across whenever I've got a spare moment."

Susan's calm exterior belied the excitement building up inside.

"Fine, that's all sorted then," said John. "I'll put it in the minutes then it's done proper. Susan to do inventory..." he said as he wrote.

"Can I have the treasurer's report please?"

Fred Pickup asserted himself:

"It's been a complicated period. All of a sudden, we're very well off. But I must warn the committee that it's a false picture. We started at the beginning of the season with a deficit of fifty-six pounds. We now have over two thousand pounds in the bank after paying Benjamin his wages. But I have to tell you that the money is a loan from Sir Alfred Bullock."

The committee members, apart from John and Susan, gasped.

"If I could come in here," said John getting to his feet quickly. "Fred and I had a quick look at the books, and it was quite clear that we weren't going to make it through the first month, let alone the season. We needed some cash in hand. So I took it on myself to sort it out. Alf

Bullock is an old friend, who has offered us cash when we were hard up in the past. On this occasion, we decided it was in the club's best interest to accept his offer. If we lost Benjamin because we couldn't pay him, we'd be knackered for the rest of the season. Don't forget we need to win something."

John paused.

There was a silence that suggested indecision in the minds of the rest of the committee. Susan looked round and sensed the dilemma.

"Well, I'd like to offer my thanks to John and Fred who have used their initiative to prevent the potential closure of the club."

The others, grateful for the influence, followed suit.

"Yes, yes, well done," they added, stopping just short of cheering.

When the plaudits had ceased, Janice raised her hand.

"It's right to praise them. But what I can't understand is how, after all the wages have been paid and all the other expenditure, we still have so much money in the bank. All we've had is one karaoke night and borrowed two thousand pounds."

Fred leapt in: "I'll gladly go through the accounts with you," he offered, in the hope that she would decline. "It's very complex and this is neither the time nor the place. But I can assure you that all is in order."

"It's not that I don't trust you Fred... I'd trust you with my last penny... it's just that in simple maths..."

Fred stopped her: "We made more on the karaoke than we first thought Janice. It's as simple as that...ok?" Fred raised his voice slightly.

Janice noted his manner and backed down: "Sure, glad we've so much."

"That's the end of my report Mr Chairman. Now if we can move on... I have to go shortly."

The others stared at Fred. His raised voice was now accompanied by a twitch below his right eye.

"He's lying," thought Susan.

No one had the heart for any other business, and the meeting broke up quickly. Susan accompanied Janice through the door.

"Never seen Fred like that before," she uttered as soon as the door shut behind them.

Inside, John, Fred and Tom remained at the bar. They waited until they heard the click of the gate indicating they could not be overheard.

"Well done Fred, she never suspected a thing," said Tom grinning.

Fred didn't quite see it that way.

"This is a right friggin' how-do-you-do," he replied getting angrier. "You've got me falsifying the books, lying to Janice and lying to my wife. If she finds out, I'm dead."

Tom looked at him. "What are you lying about to your wife?"

"I told her it was darts and dominoes. I couldn't have come otherwise."

"You didn't mention the stripper then," said John, digging Fred in the ribs as he spoke.

"That's another thing! You lot lied to me. 'Exotic dancer, just like a disco,' you said."

"Bet you didn't know where to look," laughed John as the humour gained pace.

Tom put on a straight face and confronted the others.

"That bloody snake had me worried. Big bugger. What had we done, if that had got loose?"

"Send for Janice, she'd have seen it off," roared John.

"Anyway, let's get down to brass tacks. How much did we make?" asked Tom.

Fred's face cracked a smile mixed with resignation.

"It were a bit awkward to work out. Seemed to be money coming from all angles. Nobody kept a check on how many tickets we sold. I was just given a bag of cash marked tickets. I asked some if they'd paid, and they said they didn't know ~ but were quite happy to pay again. Football cards going round all night, profit from the bar, made a fortune there," he paused for a moment and the others looked at him expectantly.

"Strangest thing though, I found this old bucket with the stripper's name on it... Mainly pound coins... over hundred quid when I counted it. As she was leaving, I asked her if she wanted it. She said she'd taken all the notes but had a reputation to maintain, said wouldn't be seen dead walking the streets with a bucket of loose change."

The others roared with laughter.

"What's so funny?" Fred asked.

But the others, too busy holding their stomachs or wiping away the tears, couldn't reply.

"Anyway, we made over five hundred quid on the night," he said proudly.

"Bucket of loose change" spluttered John.

Opportunity Knocks for Susan

Benjamin had risen, as usual, just after noon. Still in a fog from the previous night's excesses, he had made his way to the cricket ground. He had a list of ground maintenance chores to perform. Within minutes of arrival, he was lazily going round and round the pitch sitting on the motor mower with his head rhythmically moving to the music playing on his headphones.

Susan, in the hallway of her house, was staring at the mirror psyching herself up for the next phase of her quest.

"No need for excuses. Plausible reason for being there. The sun is shining, so am I," she said confidently. She palmed her shorter that usual skirt down, and raised her shoulders. "Ready," she added as she shut the door behind her and purposefully strutted towards the cricket ground.

She stood on the perimeter of freshly cut grass, took a deep breath and waited for Benjamin to make his way round to her side of the pitch. As he approached, she stood pretending to write in a spiral bound notepad. She beckoned officiously as he got nearer. He veered off his route and came to rest alongside. He cut the engine of the mower and removed his headphones.

"Afternoon Mrs Perkins, is it a good day or what?" he greeted her buoyantly, not really expecting an answer to his question.

She stared at him, looked him over. She usually saw him at a distance in cricket whites, but all he had on was a sloppy t-shirt, cut-off jeans for shorts and a pair of old sandals.

Her heart pounded and she felt a droplet of perspiration make its way between her shoulder blades down the small of her back.

"No backing out now," she urged herself.

As he got closer, she stared at his big eyes, pearly white teeth and a broad beaming smile. Beads of sweat like precious stones glistened on his dark forehead. She felt her heart palpitate. His rippling muscles flexed as he climbed down off the mower.

"Good God," she muttered as she noted his huge hand deftly turn off his Walkman and remove his earplugs.

"Is you alright?" she heard him ask.

"Sorry…err…yes," she stammered.

"You seemed gone for a minute," he added smiling.

She looked up at him. The sun, being behind him, got in her eyes. She held her palm up to shield her face.

"I was wondering if you could help."

"You name it."

"I've been asked to do an inventory of the old store. Could you help me to identify some items? Won't take a minute," she said, hoping the well-rehearsed lines didn't sound too wooden.

"Sure can. Anything to keep me off that old mower, shakes my bones to bits," he said as he rummaged in his pocket. "Got the key right here." He held out a well-used key dangling from a piece of frayed string.

They walked in silence towards the white concrete garage that had adopted the name 'old store'. He opened the side door and let Susan in first. It was darker than she thought. What light there was came from whitewashed windows along one side.

"Can you see ok Mrs Perkins, or shall I open the main door?"

"No!" she shouted, louder than she meant to.

He looked at her, taken by surprise at the volume of her voice.

"It'll be fine when our eyes get adjusted," she said more softly, with just a hint of apology.

They stood for a moment. Then, as their vision improved from only registering silhouettes, to being able to see simple detail, he asked: "What's first on your list then?" He screwed up his eyes to assist his vision.

"Grass seed," she replied, putting down the pad down on a sack that clearly indicated grass seed on the label.

As he routed among the other sacks, she moved over and gingerly closed the door. Being unfamiliar, she hadn't reckoned on the metallic click of the latch.

"Hey, I can't see at all now," he announced, unaware of her intentions.

He turned to investigate and found Susan had moved over to him and was unbuttoning the top of her summer dress. Anticipating her intentions, he protested.

"Stop right there, Mrs Perkins, we're getting into very dangerous territory." There was genuine fear in his voice.

"I'll take full responsibility for any consequences," she whispered in an even softer tone.

Susan moved closer and took his hand. She was surprised how calm she was and how much he was trembling. He flinched as though it was too hot to touch.

"Relax," she encouraged. She let go of his hand and proceeded to undo the remainder of the buttons.

"We've got big, big problems if we gets caught," he cautioned. The beads of sweat on his forehead multiplied. "My job, your marriage, and the bad, bad publicity. Have you thought this out?"

"I've thought about nothing else," she said taking control. "Don't worry Benjamin, nobody's going to find out." She sensed that he was beginning to tremble a little less.

"This is fire we're playing with," he pleaded.

"Don't do it," he muttered, weakening.

"No need to worry. I won't tell if you don't," she added as her excitement began to increase.

Some time later, after Susan had showered, she wrapped the towelling robe around her and watched him through the bedroom window. He was tidying up the equipment after having marked out the pitch. He showed no outward sign of the past hour's goings on, he just carried on nodding his head to the music.

Her head, though, was still spinning.

"Bloody brilliant," she whispered. "Guilt? None so far…"

As she watched him load the wheelbarrow, she kept reliving the details of the afternoon.

"And all in proportion," she giggled.

But then within seconds, the smile faded from her face. 'Where does this leave me now? What about Geoffrey? Will I ever want him again? In some respects, I'm worse off.' She sat on the edge of the bed thinking about her predicament.

She faced the mirror on the wardrobe door and confided: "He was so strong, but unbelievably gentle. Never once did I think he'd rush. Not like Geoffrey ~ all rough and tumble and smelling of beer ~ with the statutory 'Have you finished yet?' at the end." She kept looking at the mirror, half-expecting to get an answer. A flashback in her mind recalled how it used to be with Geoffrey. "It hasn't always been bad. He was a good lover. What the hell's happened?' She turned away from the mirror and lay back on the bed. Her mind, like a video, rewound and fast-forwarded the activities.

"What now? Can't leave it like this. I know it's risky but… well, it was so… good. And it can only get better, can't it?" She shuddered as she went through it again.

"Seriously, unbelievably, very good."

A Neighbourly Drink

Geoffrey Perkins and Albert Bradley had not been neighbours long, but they had much in common. Each had come to the conclusion that living on the edge of Throttle's cricket pitch was a mistake ~ and had, as the experience of the recent weeks had shown, become intolerable. They had assessed their own particular circumstances and decided that moving house, if at all possible, would involve a considerable financial loss.

On a more domestic front, each had tasks to perform that had initially been pleasures. But as time wore on, the novelty faded, and the tasks had become tedious chores. Since the removal of his beloved garden, Albert had replaced most of the plants with plastic replicas. But on the edge of his guttering, where he thought the ball could not possibly reach, he had installed hanging baskets. These initially overflowed with fuchsias and geraniums and other species that in the past he could have cultivated with little or no bother at all. But by their very nature, hanging baskets require continuous attention. After suffering the rigours of the northern climate for only a short time, they began to look tired and bedraggled. In an effort to maintain the correct moisture content, and to ease the physical effort of lugging buckets of water up ladders, he had installed a piped watering system to each plant. The pleasure of a job well done when the system was installed, gave way to utter despair during subsequent test runs. The first plant on the piped run became deluged with water, but the last only received limited drips. 'Despondent' was becoming a word frequently used by Albert.

Next door, Geoffrey was out retrieving the day's playthings from the straggly unkempt garden. He observed the scattered remains of extortionately priced toys, left abandoned as though they were worthless. The cost of items had always been a source of interest to Geoffrey. He could, without effort, relate the once much sought-after articles to the amount of hours he worked or how many barrels of beer he would have to sell. He looked down at a pair of once smart-looking trainers.

Jesus, a full morning's work there," he muttered as he tugged them from the patch of long grass.

As he walked round, putting the broken or out-of-favour toys into a large washing basket, he noticed Albert. He was sitting on the floor with his head between his hands. He also noticed water flooding from the hanging baskets to one side of his house.

"You look like you could do with a beer," he said, as a thin stream of water made a direct path towards where Albert was sitting.

"Soddin' hell!" Albert exclaimed, as he felt the dampness creep through his trousers. He leapt up.

"A beer ~ do you want one or what?" Geoffrey repeated, but louder.

"Yes, please." Albert twisted his neck to look at the dark stain on his pants. Then, he stared at the array of beers in the boot of Geoffrey's car. "Bloody hell!" His eyes darted from one decoratively labelled bottle to another. "I've never seen these before."

Geoffrey explained the line of products.

"I'd value your opinion," he lied.

They sat on Geoffrey's steps so as to avoid the soil and plant laden stream that continued to pour down the front of Albert's house. As the sun began to set, and the alcohol began to take effect, they mellowed.

"Wife will think I've pissed myself," Albert grinned, looking at the contrasting colour on the back of his pants.

There was a pause as Albert's face slid back into a sombre expression.

"Sodding nightmare out here. No peace at weekends," he moaned.

"Not much we can do though," sighed Geoffrey.

"Not exactly true ~ not now that your missus is in with them," he replied, with a slight slur to his voice.

"What do you mean?"

"I just heard that she's joined the committee," said Albert, choosing his words more carefully and wondering why he had a problem pronouncing 'committee.'

"My wife's offered to help, that's all. Make tea and sandwiches. Nowt wrong with that is there?"

"You mean she's not trying to *infiltrate* them?" said Albert winking strangely.

"Infiltrate? She's not a bleeding spy. She just wants to help out," he responded, trying not to raise his voice.

"Don't get me wrong. It's just that it'd be an ideal opportunity to find out what their strategies are."

"Strategies, what sodding strategies?"

"They must have a strategy to get a Cup. They need one, otherwise the ground goes back to the landlord... he wants it for building land. The good news is we could flit, no problem."

Geoffrey looked up and smiled.

"Flit eh... we've err a brand new one, just come out. You can tell me what you think?"

Geoffrey rummaged amongst other bottles in the back of the car. He held them out and flicked off the tops with his thumbs. As the froth poured on to the floor, he said:

"Go on then, how?"

"Simple," said Albert, belching back the gas from the beer. "All we have to do is stop these bastards from winning a Cup."

He indicated towards the pitch using the bottle as a pointer.

"You can't do that. It's unethical… illegal… You can't stop somebody winning… can you?"

"We have to do something ~ so that I can retire and go back to being a happy man, not a miserable bastard like I am now." Albert started to fill up. "Jesus now look at me, we 'ave to do something." He routed for a hanky in his damp trousers.

Albert didn't go out much these days, and the nearest he came to drinking alcohol was sipping his wife's sloe gin in measured amounts. So as the effect of Old Goat's Horn kicked in, his voice got louder and his language stronger. Through a tear-soaked hanky he ranted at Geoffrey.

"So you'd rather stay here forever, being battered by bleedin' cricket balls and living in negative bleedin equity, would you? Well you've got three months to do something, or it's another ten long soddin' years."

Geoffrey leaned forward and put a hand over Albert's mouth, hushing him, and looking round.

"Keep your voice down. Ok, go on then…" Geoffrey urged.

They huddled together, but Albert had by now lost the ability to speak intelligibly and Geoffrey began to lose the will to listen.

Shortly after, Geoffrey was supporting Albert with one arm round his waist while he rang the front door bell.

"Sorry Mrs Bradley, didn't mean this to happen," he said, as he helped Albert inside.

Later, Albert recounted to his wife how all of a sudden his legs would no longer support him, and his tongue appeared to have doubled in size.

"See you've made a big hit with the neighbours," said Susan when Geoffrey finally came to bed.

"Don't you start! You said you were just going to help out with the teas. Apparently, you're making a name for yourself as Little Miss Know-it-all."

No other communication occurred that night. The only link between them was the stretched material of the duvet as they slept back to back.

New Day Dawns

The sun was shining and the birds were singing as Sir Alf whizzed down the country lane on the outskirts of the village. Being able to feel the wind in his face was all brand new.

'Should have done this years ago,' he mused. 'But what's done is done.' His new 'GT' chair, as he now called it, had given him back some of the independence that he enjoyed before the accident. Each time out, he would venture further and further afield. He had got used to the new chair's handling, but as the novelty of the neck-snapping acceleration and tyre-screeching brakes wore off, he very rarely used it to its full potential.

He was savouring the peace and solitude from a viewpoint overlooking the moors, when he was interrupted by his other aid to autonomy. As he fumbled to get at the melodic buzzing of his mobile phone (which unfortunately for the other backpackers and picnickers, happened to be buried at the bottom of his panniers) he apologised to all within earshot.

"Sorry, sorry. It's under my sandwiches."

They were not impressed.

"Come out for a bit of peace. What's he want to bring that thing for?" mumbled a rambler, his map case fluttering in the breeze. When Sir Alf answered in his usual loud voice, a group of picnickers packed up and moved on, letting him know their feelings on the subject of modern communications.

"Shouldn't be allowed, should be banned," said an elderly but hardy lady, pulling her hood over her head.

"It's Terry Cargill here, can you hear me?"

"Yes, loud and clear," Alf responded.

Another group of picnickers nodded in agreement. "We can all bloody hear you!" they shouted.

Sir Alf sensed their displeasure and whispered into the receiver.

"I'll get back to you, five minutes." He pressed the off button and apologised again to the few who remained.

In a gate hole further down the lane, he dialled Terry Cargill's number by selecting the memory button. When he bought the phone, the instructions advised that up to fifty numbers could be stored on its memory. Up to now he only had five, indicative, he thought, of how empty his existence had become.

"Is that you Alf? Reception's not so good," said Terry, speaking slowly.

"What have you got for me?" asked Sir Alf.

"Well it's like this: apparently you signed over all the managerial responsibility to your Roland for the duration of your incapacity."

"Meaning what?"

"Well I suppose it depends on your interpretation of the word, 'incapacity'."

"You mean that although I'm sound in me head, because I'm in a wheelchair I'm considered incapacitated?"

"Something like that... Have you had physio?" asked Terry, trying to be helpful.

"You need some feeling, some sensation, something for them to work with... apparently," Sir Alf replied, his voice beginning to taper off. "Thanks anyway. I'll be in touch."

He made his way back up the hill to the viewpoint. This time, he made sure the phone was switched off. He stared out across the hills. It had all the ingredients of a scenic landscape painting, but all he could see was bankruptcy and permanent disablement.

A brightly dressed rambler nearby was pouring his similarly dressed wife a cup of steaming tea from a flask. As they dunked their biscuits, she looked at him and smiled.

"Grand to be alive isn't it," she mused wistfully, in a voice that carried.

He looked in their direction, and then set off home.

He entered the front door to be confronted by Flora vacuuming the hall carpet.

"You still here?" he queried.

"I'll go now if you want."

"Sorry, I've had a bad day, fancy a coffee?" he apologised.

"But you set off happy as Larry. What happened?" she asked.

"I've had a call from my solicitor. The bottom line is this: if I remain in this chair much longer, our Roland will bankrupt the lot of us."

Flora poured the hot water into the mugs.

"Seems strange to have your own son, who you see most mornings, in a position that he can ruin you.

Have you tried talking to him? Surely he can see sense if..."

"It's like this: I made him the boss, and now he thinks he knows best and rides roughshod over anybody who says different. I've tried talking to him from all angles ~ as a father, as a businessman, as a friend even. Just ends in a row. Then he says, I should look after myself and let him get on with running the business. Well, we only agreed that he could run the show 'while I'm incapacitated'. In other words, stuck in this frigging chair. Thing is, according to the doctors, I should be well on my way by now, but nowt seems to be happening. No feeling... see."

As if to demonstrate, he slapped the top of his leg: "Nothing."

"You have to believe in what the doctors say. You might just have to wait a bit longer, that's all," Flora said, unconvincingly.

"In the meantime the mill goes down the pan," Sir Alf said more abruptly than he intended. "And now Miriam's buggered off. Found a note on the side this morning. No details, just buggered off."

They drank the coffee in silence, both too busy with their own thoughts.

Susan Has Her Say

Arthur Padstow read out the minutes of the last meeting and asked for a seconder. Without hesitation or consideration, Tom Deakin raised his hand, and then went back to his conversation with Fred Pickup about it being the longest day and how from now on the nights would start to draw in.

Susan raised her hand: "Point of order Mr Chairman."

The conversation stopped and everyone looked up.

"The minutes are a legally binding document. Proper regard should be given to them. The impression I get is that they're only being given cursory consideration."

"What are you suggesting?" barked Tom.

"All I'm saying is that when you seconded those minutes, you hardly looked up from your chat."

Tom immediately stood up, threw the agenda across the table, and announced: "I don't have to put up with this crap. I resign. Get yourselves another grounds man."

The rest, including Susan, looked aghast as he slammed the door behind him. John Appleby's plea of, "Tom, Tom, oh Tom," went unheard.

Janice turned on him: "This is your fault. You've as much idea about running a meeting as I don't know what. If you'd kept a tighter rein in the past, this wouldn't have happened."

Arthur, now inflamed, chipped in: "Excuse me, are you saying that we don't take these meetings seriously? That's an insult after all the unpaid hours I've put in. Let's see how you manage on your own then." He too, threw the agenda on the table, and left.

"This is all down to you," Janice said pointing at John. Then, as her eyes filled with tears: "Look what you've done now."

She got out a tissue and wiped her eyes, smearing mascara across her face. She looked at the blackened tissue, then in the tiny mirror in her handbag. "I can't stay, not like this." She duly grabbed her coat and left.

Fred and John stared at Susan.

"Happy now?" said Fred.

Susan stared at the table.

"No point continuing. We're not quorate. Think I'll grab a pint where there's less aggro," said John wearily.

"I'm sorry, I just thought that…"

"Don't worry love, they'll come back," said John putting on his coat.

"After you've apologised that is," said Fred icily.

"Take no notice, there's been a bit of pressure this year. Folk are a bit on edge. This Roland Bullock business is getting on us nerves," said John, trying to ease her feelings.

As Susan entered the hallway, Geoffrey ~ not taking his eyes from the TV ~ unknowingly poured salt into the wound: "You're home early, did you sack them all?"

Susan ignored the comment and went straight into the kitchen. She flicked the top off one of his free samples and drank from the bottle.

Flora Does Some Research

Flora had spread the library books out on the kitchen table and was leafing through them. She loved the aroma of the ink as she opened each page, irrespective of what was printed. She was determined to help Sir Alf in some way. She flipped open a page at random. It opened on a picture of massage techniques, applied to a scantily clad lady.

"If it's stimulation you want!" she grinned. Then, she shut the book as she heard her mother's footsteps coming down the hall. She entered the kitchen and scanned the array of books. Her mother had got used to her unpredictable ways.

"What you up to now?" said her mother impatiently.

"Oh hello Flora, have you had a nice day?" Flora retaliated.

They were getting off to yet another bad start.

"What's this, another fad? Like being a vegetarian, then craving bacon sandwiches. Or condemn the French, but eating their apples."

As she spotted the titles of her daughter's latest obsession, she was almost lost for words. She opened a well-thumbed page to reveal a naked couple in the process of reciprocal manipulation.

"*Aromatherapy for Beginners, Full Body Massage Techniques,* Don't let your dad see these, he'll go bloody mad. What do you want these for anyway?"

"Because I'm interested in it, ok?" Flora slammed the heavyweight book shut. "Look, they do this at night school. It can't be iffy, if they do it at night school."

Flora gathered the books and marched towards the door:

"Whatever I'm interested in, you've got a problem with it."

Flora's mum had been here before. 'Piggy in the middle again,' she thought as Flora went on. Then she heard herself repeating similar lines to the ones she always used: "He only wants what's best for you. Doesn't want you getting into trouble. If he sees books like these, he'll get the wrong idea!"

Flora thumped up the stairs and slammed her bedroom door.

Her mother stared at the kettle that seemed to refuse to boil, and pondered. 'I'm defending the soddin' bigot and he's not even here. I never used to be like this.' She sniffed back a tear as the kettle's whistle got louder. She blew her nose on a piece of floral kitchen towel, and then reached for the comfort of the biscuit barrel.

Susan Applies Some Pressure

Susan approached the reception desk in Joseph Lagg Estate Agents. She had already had a look at the boards containing details of properties in the area, particularly the ones on the border of the cricket pitch.

"This has been here a while," she said, pointing at one to see the reaction.

Julia, the receptionist looked up and gave a rehearsed response:

"Not much moving. Things aren't as bad as last year. Would you like to see inside?"

"Not now thanks. I've just popped in to see Mr Lagg."

"He's busy with a client, but shouldn't be much longer... been in an hour now."

It was then that Susan spotted the personal number plate on the new Jaguar outside the shop.

"RB1. Posh car," she pried.

"Yes, it's Mr Bullock's. All right isn't it?"

"Roland Bullock?"

"Yes, colleague of Mr Lagg."

Susan made herself comfortable in the little waiting area.

"You'll wait then?" inquired Julia.

Susan looked up from the 'Horse and Hound' magazine, provided to lift the tone of the area.

"Oh yes," she replied crisply.

Julia pressed down the button on the antique communication system.

"Sorry to disturb you Mr Lagg, but there's a Mrs Perkins waiting to see you."

Joe Lagg dreaded that name, and in a panic held down the speak button by mistake: "Shit! Tell her I'll be out soon."

Two customers who had just entered the office, turned around and left, while Susan grinned behind the magazine.

"I think Mrs Perkins got the message, Mr Lagg," she sighed.

Behind the brick wall, Roland was preparing to leave:

"Ah... this is the lady who puts the fear of God into you. Better not keep *her* waiting then."

In the reception area, Roland and Susan momentarily stared at one another. Then, they quickly looked away, neither wanting to give away any clues.

Joe stood in the doorway of his office, watching as Roland climbed into his car.

"Come in Mrs Perkins, always good to see you. Coffee?"

Susan did not mince her words: "Come across the word 'hypocrite' in your crossword recently?"

"What's that supposed to mean?"

"Good to see you Mrs Perkins," mimicked Susan.

"All right, all right, it's just that the market's a bit slow and you want your problem solving right now. It might take a bit longer than we thought," he said, unable to make eye contact.

"Bullshit!" snapped Susan angrily. "You've done nothing to sort this out. You ripped us off at the start and now you're just stalling."

Joe pushed a coffee cup and a plate of biscuits towards her.

"That's not true. Things are happening. I know it's not obvious, but things are happening behind the scenes."

"Ok, tell me what you're doing then."

"I can't. It'd be betraying a confidence. But you have my word that it'll be sorted."

Susan sipped her coffee.

"Your word! How can I trust someone who swindles you in the first place, then won't explain how he plans to sort it?"

"Just trust me."

"How long before things happen?"

"Couple of weeks, maybe three."

Susan picked up a Bourbon from the plate.

"Dubious friends you've got," she said, through a mouth full of crumbs.

"That wasn't a friend, it was a colleague. And that's my business!" he snapped defensively.

"Touchy! But how did you know I was referring to Roland Bullock? See you in a fortnight."

Susan grinned and strutted out.

As Julia cleared the cups, she smiled mischievously. She leaned over his shoulder then half-whispered:

"Just how much does she know?"

An Apologetic Albert Bradley

Albert Bradley gently rapped the knocker of the Perkins household. He had been working himself up to the visit for a couple of days and had been practising the wording of his apology most of the afternoon.

"I'll get it!" shouted Geoffrey.

As the door opened, Albert tried to smile but failed. He couldn't remember ever having apologised to anyone before. He certainly hadn't smiled properly for years, so the next few minutes were going to be a bit of a challenge.

"I've come about the other night. Don't know what came over me." The words felt like broken glass in his throat.

"Not a problem," grinned Geoffrey.

"I'd have come sooner, but I've been ill for days. Couldn't stop shaking, retching all the first night, then dizzy spells. Bleedin awful taste and gas… Jesus, banished to the garden at one point." Albert held his head and his backside as he explained.

"Some hangover, eh? Fancy a drink?" Geoffrey laughed, exhibiting zero sympathy. "That Old Goat's Horn, what a cracker!"

"You're very kind, but tea will do nicely," said Albert holding his stomach as though he could feel rumblings.

They sat at the kitchen table and drank tea, though Albert spilled most of his, as he still had not got rid of the shakes.

"Sorry," he apologised, as the tea formed a puddle round his cup.

"Never mind that. This business with the cricket club. Run it by me again," said Geoffrey, wiping the table.

Albert looked up: "In a nutshell, the club has to win a Cup. If they can't, the ground goes back to the Bullocks. They build houses on it, and we get the going rate for ours."

"Seems a bit much to have our house prices resting on whether a team wins or not."

"Precisely," said Albert.

"But you can't help the other teams win, can you?" queried Geoffrey.

"No, but maybe you can prevent Throttle from winning." Albert's face changed to a sinister leer. "It's like this. We have to ensure that at vital stages of certain matches, things happen that prevent play continuing. Or we could see to it that vital players aren't fit, or are called away, or sommat." Albert's grin turned to a beaming smile.

"Sounds decidedly dodgy, if you ask me ~ 'specially if someone, not a million miles away, finds out."

Geoffrey nodded towards the living room. Susan, engrossed in a televised 'who done it' was unaware of the shenanigans being plotted in her own kitchen.

"If she ever finds out, we're dead meat. And I mean stone cold, on the slab, dead meat," Albert cautioned. "But it's half the market price of your house or their Cup. What's it to be?"

Teacups clashed across the kitchen table as they toasted their new alliance. "Cobblers to the cricket," they harmonised in hushed tones. But their faces turned to horror when they heard Susan's voice.

"Not sure if I approve of grown men whispering in kitchens. You'll be wearing funny outfits next."

"Not up to anything," said Geoffrey.

"Didn't say you were. Sounds like somebody's got a guilty conscience. How's your head Albert? I believe you've been ill. Stopped farting have you? Something in Old Goat's Horn, Geoffrey does nothing else."

She didn't wait for a reply, just smirked, grabbed the biscuit box and returned to watch the second part of her film.

They sat motionless in the kitchen, and then Geoffrey nodded towards the back door. Once outside, he gently closed it.

"What do you reckon?" asked Albert, thumbing towards the closed door.

Geoffrey shrugged his shoulders. "Not a clue any more mate," he sighed.

Rest and Recuperation

The following Saturday, Geoffrey arrived home after plying his ale samples. On the basis of his reasonable success, he decided to test his product for quality and performance. Recently, he had wallowed in the delights of being a couch potato. The few hours of doing 'what the hell I like' while Susan and Alison were at the cricket had become a refuge from the mayhem of work, and he was sorry to say, the bedlam of home.

He wasn't a keen football supporter, but he enjoyed a game with lots of action. If there was a good film on the other channel, he would flick between the two, to double the entertainment. He had tried to develop the skill of flicking between three stations, but this taxed his limited concentration. On more than one occasion, he had been found fast asleep, bottle and remote control still gripped firmly in his hands.

He had settled down to a second-rate film and athletics, neither of which could overcome the soporific effect of the beer, when he was rudely plucked from his semi-slumber. Although it was only Susan and Alison returning early, to Geoffrey it sounded like a cross between an angry mob and a herd of cattle charging down the hallway.

"What the bleedin' hell's going on?" he remarked as they flew straight past him and entered the kitchen.

"They could have killed him, killed all of them for that matter," wailed Susan.

Peeved as he was at the intrusion, he thought it sensible to inquire about the apparent attempted murder.

"Killed who?" he inquired, poking his head round the kitchen door.

"Ben, Ben... for goodness sake, who else?" yelled Susan.

Geoffrey looked at Alison and mouthed: "Who's Ben?"

Alison, taking after her mother, was also devoid of patience.

"Daddy, don't you know anything? It's Benjamin... Benjamin's been hurt."

Geoffrey had been harbouring unpleasant suspicions about Benjamin and subsequently cared little for his welfare. So, as his sincerity faded away, he could only offer a crass comment.

"Slip on the grass did he?"

They looked daggers at him. Susan pulled Alison towards her, put her hands over her ears, and hissed: "You bastard, they could have died. Didn't you see the ambulance?"

Geoffrey's brain raced. 'Beginning to lose this one,' he thought.

He had learned to think quickly in situations like this, situations that unfortunately were becoming more common. He immediately disposed of stating the actual reason ~ 'I didn't see the ambulance or its flashing blue light because I was horizontal in an alcoholic stupor.' So he went for the 'feigning compassion' routine.

Holding out his palms and employing a pained expression, he said: "So what on earth's happened?"

"Someone tried to kill the team!" shouted Alison, basking in the hysteria.

Geoffrey, still not convinced and unable to resist putting his foot in it again, added, "Aren't we exaggerating a bit here? After all, I haven't heard any bombs going off."

He looked at their dumbstruck faces and offered a watery smile.

"They were poisoned, you idiot!" said Susan.

Geoffrey screwed up his face in disbelief.

"On a cricket pitch? How?"

"They came out after tea, and within minutes some couldn't see. Benjamin was holding his throat because he couldn't breath. The match had to be abandoned."

"So who made the tea then?" he asked, hesitantly.

"Me and three other ladies. We've already had this inquiry. If it'd been the food, both teams would've gone down and most of the spectators. As it happens, only half our team were affected. Someone poisoned them."

There was a moment's silence, and then Susan asked the question that Geoffrey was dying to pose.

"Who'd want to poison our own team?"

"Can't think. Was it an important game?" he tentatively asked, with an excited tremor creeping into his voice.

Alison gave him the answer he was waiting for: "They were playing the top of the league."

"So what happens to the points? Do they split them? Are they lost or do they have to play again?" asked Geoffrey, then realised he had overstepped the mark.

Susan stared at him in disbelief. "Have you no feelings? People are nearly killed and all you can ask about is the points. Get your coat Alison."

"Where are you going?" he asked.

"We're going visiting. He's being kept in for observation."

As the door slammed, Geoffrey grabbed another bottle, settled down on the sofa and pondered.

"Well done Albert, I don't know how you did it, but well done."

The Day After The Poisoning

At The Ram Inn, normal Sunday discussions gave way to the events of the previous day.

"Bastards should be hung," remarked a local.

"Hanging's too good. They should be burnt at the stake with their entrails hanging…"

People moved away from the individual who harboured sadistic inclinations.

At the rear of the pub, Roland, Joe and the Jakeson brothers sipped their beer in quiet reflection.

"You could have killed them, you stupid bastard. If they find out, we're on porridge," hissed Joe.

"Keep your voice down. There's a soddin' lynch mob over there," Roland mumbled. He tried not to stare at the rough, unshaven gentlemen at the bar, who, in his mind would have no problem stringing those responsible for the poisoning from the rafters, then totally unconcerned would continue with his drinking.

Feeling aggrieved at the lack of appreciation for a job well done, Reginald Jakeson made no apologies, "You said hinder play, prevent them winning."

Joe, who was getting angrier by the minute and could have sworn he could taste porridge, replied, "Hinder play, we said. Prevent them winning, we also said. We did not say friggin' kill them!"

Simon, who, as the years advanced was becoming more and more like the character in the nursery rhyme, offered a comment: "How was we to know he'd lick the ball?"

Roland and Joe stared at them. Then, in unison, they urged, "Go on."

"Reginald kept the umpire talking while I stole the ball out of his pocket. It were right easy," explained Simon.

"They keep hold of it during tea to prevent tampering. Ironic like," added Reginald.

"I painted it, put it under the drier in the gents, then put it back."

Roland looked puzzled. "Let me get this right. You painted it. What with? emulsion?"

"No, it were a mixture of black cap mushrooms, nettle and laburnum leaves, put in a blender then sieved. It's the clear liquid that's painted on," Reginald explained.

"Where'd you get this from ~ a frigging witch doctor?" Roland spat out in exasperation.

"No, our mum uses it."

"Your mum uses it! What the hell for? Getting rid of the neighbours? Euthanasia?"

Simon looked at Reginald: "Euthy what?"

"Killing old folk," he clarified.

Reginald turned to the others.

"She puts it on the fence to keep the cats out."

"And does it?" asked Joe.

"Oh yes, they never come back," he smiled.

Joe held his head in his hands. "That's because they're all friggin' dead. They don't come back because they're dead. Jesus, what have I got mixed up with here?"

"It were only supposed to make 'em itch and their eyes water ~ only the pro went and licked the ball... Game *were* abandoned though," said Reginald positively.

"That's because there weren't enough players left to play," Joe said, head still in hands.

"You were lucky this time. We just want you to be more careful, that's all. Basically we're pleased with what you've done, but you have to be more subtle," Roland said.

He got up and left without finishing his beer.

Joe felt the need for anaesthetic from the day's events and ordered another beer. He left Reginald explaining the word 'subtle' to Simon.

"It's how mothers feed their babies, but I haven't sussed the connection yet. Strange bloke that Roland."

Joe, beginning to despair, turned to watch the big match on the widescreen that had been reinstated to lure back the locals.

Later that afternoon, Albert was washing his car in the drive. Stooping to rinse the sponge, he got the feeling he was being watched. Turning to one side, he noticed Geoffrey standing at the living room window. Immediately they made eye contact, Geoffrey started winking and making exaggerated thumbs-up gestures. Albert, unaware of what he was getting at, shrugged his shoulders.

Minutes later, Geoffrey was standing at the fence. "Well done Albert," he said excitely, in a low voice.

"Well done what?"

Albert was grumpy at being disturbed from another task he had come to detest.

"It was you, wasn't it?"

"What was me?" He was starting to feel agitated.

"It was you who poisoned the team and got the game called off."

"What do you think I am, an effing serial killer? Do you think I'd poison the whole team just to get the match stopped?" Albert waved a dripping sponge. "You must have a poor impression of me if you think I'd do a thing like that."

He walked towards the tap in the garage.

Geoffrey's head dropped: "Sorry Albert, should have known better."

Albert turned off the tap while Geoffrey, standing in the garage opening, scratched his head in a vain attempt to get his brains cells working.

"So who… who'd kill the whole team to stop the game?" he wondered aloud. He hadn't a clue. He looked up to see Albert with that fiendish expression on his face, the same as the other night in the kitchen.

"It doesn't follow that whoever did it wanted to kill the whole team. Maybe they only wanted to kill one person, but as a cover up, they were prepared to kill them all."

Geoffrey, not convinced, but not wanting to hurt his feelings tempered his comment: "Seems a trifle extreme! So who?"

"Could be anyone. Could be any husband wanting to get even with the pro," he smirked. Albert, exaggerating the part of a fishwife, beckoned him over. "I've heard that wherever the pro plays, he has it away with any number of women, and there's a horde of angry husbands just waiting for the right moment. You never know, it could be a bloke from round here. Apparently he's had his share of this village already."

Geoffrey stared at him glumly. He mused over Albert's comments for the rest of the day, his mind veering from one scene to the next. Susan's apparent familiarity, the episode where the pro had carried her into the house, her mood swings, the lack of affection. In Geoffrey's mind, it all added up to the unthinkable. 'Keep calm. Get to the bottom of it, but don't put your foot in it.' The mixed metaphors made him smile. He hadn't felt much like smiling recently, what with one thing and another.

"Jesus!" he shouted, his voice echoing in the empty house.

Susan and Alison had gone back to the hospital, and he now began to regret the offhand comment he threw down the hallway as they left. "Off to visit the sick are you," the words uncontrollably tripping from his tongue.

Recently he had started to think out loud, offer his problems to inanimate objects. It helped in some ways get the problem out in the open, but answers were a rarity.

He stood in front of the hall mirror and pleaded his case: "All this pressure. New job, new house, deadlines to keep. No support, no cuddles, no sex."   He paused, grabbed imaginary lapels, and gesticulated as if in a courtroom. "I'm a simple man. I don't crave horny perverted sex, just ordinary regular sex. I can't go on like this for much longer." He paused again. "I drink a bit, and it's been made clear this is frowned upon. I don't smoke. So how is a man supposed to get rid of his tension other than beer or sex? I'm not getting my share of the latter!" he bellowed. "I rest my case."

Then, a movement caught his eye. He turned to the front door and observed the distorted facial features of his wife and daughter as they pressed against the frosted glass.

Holding open the front door, he inquired: "How is he then?"

From the kitchen, Susan replied: "Better than you, from what I've just seen!"

The Brewery

Anthony Dawes and Geoffrey Perkins were having a progress meeting at the Old Goat Brewery. They sat opposite one another. As Geoffrey recounted to his wife each Monday evening, 'progress' related to "how much have you sold?"

Anthony Dawes opened proceedings: "So what's the verdict? Are the targets achievable?"

A simple "No" would have been the correct answer. But Geoffrey, not wanting to appear defeatist, used his usual logic in this all-too-familiar situation, and lied.

"Of course, just got to get round a few more clubs. Once they try out the freebies they're hooked."

"What's the general feeling about the new brew?" Anthony inquired.

"There's no doubting the punters like the taste. It's just that it's so strong, they can't remember what they've had," Geoffrey advised leaning back on his chair.

"Always been a problem with strong ale. Never mind, you seem to be shifting 'em ok, but we haven't had many large orders yet."

In reality, most clubs were afraid to have the strong brew on the premises. "We'd love to, but they start knocking lumps out of one another. We heard what happened at Throttle," was the usual reply to his sales patter.

Geoffrey was in fact drinking most of the freebies himself, so it was a curious but timely moment when fate took the shape of the local policeman and a man from the Environmental Health Department.

"Sorry to interrupt. Can we have a word?"

The policeman's massive frame dwarfed the doorway. He ducked down to avoid the top of the doorframe with his helmet.

"Course you can, what's up?" stuttered Anthony.

"We're investigating the incident at the cricket club," said the policeman, his voice sounding more formal.

"Why, what's happened?" Anthony turned to Geoffrey: "Do you know owt about this?"

Geoffrey opened his mouth to speak, but was cut off by the man from the council.

"We're here to investigate the alleged poisoning of several members of the Throttle Cricket Club team, particularly one Mr Benjamin Winston who required hospitalisation."

"Hospitalisation?" repeated Anthony.

"Witnesses have stated that Mr Winston drank at least two bottles of beer, supplied by yourselves, prior to going back on the pitch. He subsequently fell ill with a throat condition from which he nearly died."

Anthony and Geoffrey stared at one another. Then Anthony let loose: "Are you saying that our ale poisoned him?"

"We're not saying anything at the moment, other than we are investigating the incident. Therefore, anything he consumed prior to becoming ill, is under inquiry," added the man officiously.

"We've sold hundreds of bottles and no complaints… Isn't that right, Geoffrey?" Anthony said.

They all looked in Geoffrey's direction. His mind raced for an answer. This would be the second occasion, within minutes, where he pondered the consequences of telling the truth. He hesitated no longer.

"Hundreds! Not one complaint."

"That's very good to hear. But until your beer gets the 'all clear', we're putting a prohibition order on it. In other words, you're not allowed to sell any more. We'll also need a sample from the same batch."

Anthony, shocked, rose from his chair: "And you'll help us with the overdraft, go see the bank manager about the cash flow, will you? This is a business we're trying to run here, not a frigging Mickey Mouse shop. We can't afford to stop production just like that."

The policeman nodded to the man from the council, then spoke, "Don't make this more difficult than it already is, Sir. If you could let us have the samples, we'll be on our way. The quicker we get them tested, the sooner you get back in production…"

"How long?" Anthony sighed.

"A day or two at most."

Anthony slumped back in his chair. "Sort them out will you Geoffrey."

Geoffrey smiled and led them out. "This way gents. Fancy a pint before you go? We've got a new brew just finished clearing… absolutely gorgeous it is."

That evening, after Susan had listened to Geoffrey's account of the day, she received a call from John Appleby.

"I wonder if you could attend an emergency meeting?" he said, sounding like a man suffering from sleep deprivation.

"Well, yes," she replied, surprised to be asked back. "But won't you be a bit short-handed, after all the resignations?"

"Well no, not really, everyone will be there."

"So have they all taken back their notices to quit?"

"Well, yes and no…" he dithered. "Actually, I phoned them all up and asked them to come back, pleaded really. I had to, and they all agreed."

"What, just like that?" she said with disbelief.

"Well, not just like that," he paused, and took in a breath of air. "I promised them that you'd apologise. We'd have gone belly up. No grounds man, no treasurer, no tea lady. I had no choice, I'm sorry, I really am."

"You're sorry! Sounds like it's going to be me that's sorry. So what've you told them?" she said, more amused than annoyed.

"All I've said is that you're sorry you overreacted, that's all. Anyway, meetings at half seven."

"I'll be there, but don't expect sackcloth and ashes." She held the receiver as it clicked and went dead. "Bastard," she muttered.

An Extraordinary Meeting

The atmosphere was somewhat chilly as the committee members took to their seats.

John opened proceedings: "I'm sorry to do this to you on a free night, but as you can appreciate these are extenuating circumstances."

He took off his glasses, rubbed his face and then, with an audible sigh continued: "I'd also like to say that at the previous meeting I think feelings and tensions were running high. If we can all agree to let bygones be bygones, then we can get down to the proper business of what the hell happened last Saturday."

Susan had thought about what she might say at the meeting ever since the phone call. She had the intention of calling them all "spineless bastards who couldn't run a piss-up in a brewery" before tipping over the table and walking out giving them the 'V' sign.

In the end, she did what she had to do in order to maintain contact with Benjamin. She consoled herself that half an hour in the hut with Benjamin more than compensated for putting up with these moaning bastards once a month.

Through gritted teeth, she purposefully addressed the chairman without making eye contact with the others: "I'd just like to say Mr Chairman, that I apologise to all concerned for any offence caused by my overreaction at the last meeting."

The others, grateful to hear the remorse, thawed out.

"Aye lass, we all regret what happened," said Tom Deakin who then grinned and stood up. "Mind if I have a pint? It's thirsty work this apologising. Anyone else?"

Having broken the ice, everyone returned to the table with full glasses. John resumed the meeting.

"Things have taken on a great pace today what with the police and everything. Bottom line is they've interviewed Janice and the ladies who helped at the match. They seem to have been given the 'all clear'. Bloody common sense to me, everyone ate the same. They've checked the supplier of the meat and the temperature of our fridge and it's ok."

He looked round for responses but none came.

"Next item then. I'll be as tactful as I can, so bear with me."

He looked straight at Susan: "Susan," he said pointedly.

Susan, who had started to drift away from the proceedings, sat up with a start. Her mind raced. 'I've been spotted coming out of the shed. Benjamin's said something. Broken marriage, scandal, divorce.' Perspiration formed on her forehead.

"What?" she snapped.

Taken aback by the volume of her reply, he added: "Don't take it personal."

Susan butted in: "For God's sake, what?"

"The beer he drank. It were your Geoffrey's."

"Oh, that," she said. She had been readying herself to own up to the affair and to telling them not to poke their noses into her business.

"Jesus!" she sighed.

"I know it's bad news for Geoffrey," he apologised. "But we have no option but to ban it till the source of the poisoning is found."

"Point of order Mr Chairman, point of order," Tom Deakin interrupted. "I must protest at this miscarriage of justice here."

Janice turned to the chairman, screwed up her face in disbelief and mouthed silently, "Miscarriage of justice?"

Tom, sensing his supply of freebies was about to dry up offered himself as a witness for the defence.

"Your Geoffrey supplied the beer that morning: a six pack for the pro and another to be put behind the bar for emergencies. The pro has consumed part of his allocation, I've consumed most of the emergency stock."

The others smiled at his confession.

"Other than the usual," he went on, "there have been no adverse effects. So I think you'll have to look elsewhere for your culprit."

"There were more than the pro affected," butted in Fred, "albeit only mildly."

"You're right gentlemen, I think the police will have to look elsewhere for the poisoner. Meanwhile, we can't sell it or even give it away. Any remaining stock will have to be quarantined."

He mischievously grinned and gazed at Tom who in turn was staring at the remaining three bottles on the bar.

"Next item. We're only seven games away from the end of the season. We're fifth in the league and still in the Cup run. But with Ben temporarily out of the frame, we might have to get another pro. I'm afraid Bullock's axe still hangs over us."

A Quiet Breakfast?

Sir Alf and Roland were having breakfast. They had moved on from continuous rowing, to eating in total silence. Neither wanted to be in the other's company for long and so, what used to be a relaxed three quarters of an hour, was now a hasty munch of toast, a gulp of coffee and through the door. On this occasion Sir Alf was leafing through the mid-week version of The Throttle Flyer. He read out the headline with disbelief. *Big Ben Struck ~ Poisoner* **Sought.**

"Don't pull any punches this editor." Then he read out the details. "Attempted murder, perhaps by someone who harbours a grudge. What the hell is this world coming to?"

Thinking there had been a major incident that he was unaware of, Roland pricked up his ears.

"Someone's tried to poison the whole bloody cricket team. Good Jesus, mass murder right here in Throttle!" he said, forgetting his resolve never to speak in Roland's presence.

On hearing this, the coffee Roland was about to swallow took a detour and went down the wrong way. Moments later, it came back through his nose. He grabbed a serviette and held it to his face as he found himself convulsing and losing control. Sir Alf looked over the top of his paper as his son tried to regain his composure. Roland excused himself from the table and left with tears of coffee rolling down his cheeks.

Sir Alf started to read the article again when Flora entered.

"Has Master Roland finished?" she inquired looking down at the mess on the table.

"Let's just say he couldn't keep it down," he replied not taking his eyes off the article. "Have you heard about the poisoning?"

He was fully aware that she was the font of all knowledge when it came to sordid goings on.

"Shocking business, pro nearly died and the others nearly blinded. They still don't know what caused it. There's talk about revenge, you know. Somebody had it in for the pro."

He looked at her, and squinted. "Really? All this going on in a poky place like this."

"It has to happen somewhere, so it might as well be here," she grinned.

Roland, who had by now recovered and changed his shirt, was eavesdropping at the breakfast room door.

"Great," he quietly applauded, "Revenge motive… why didn't *I* think of that?"

Flora and Sir Alf turned their heads sharply as they heard the front door slam shut.

"Strange one, that," he said, with an air of disappointment.

Flora thought it best not to ask, so she just nodded as she cleaned the table. But Sir Alf didn't wait to be asked.

"Funny things kids. Thought I did all the right things for him, and look how he's turned out. Got to the point where we hardly speak."

Flora nodded continuously.

"The way he reacted, you'd think he had sommat to do with it."

"Never!" Flora said, whilst folding the sodden tablecloth.

"Crikey! Fancy thinking my own son could do a thing like that!"

"Roland wouldn't dream of it," added Flora trying to disguise her true thoughts. "Come on it's a brilliant day. Fancy a walk?"

She glanced through the window, and then realised what she had just said. "You know what I mean. I'll come with you if you like," she added sheepishly, looking at the floor.

"Aye, let's get some fresh air. I'll see you in the hallway."

A stiff breeze aided their steps as they crunched down the drive. Then, turning sharp right away from the village, the wind blew in their faces and brought tears to their eyes.

"This'll get rid of the cobwebs," said Sir Alf searching in his pocket for his hanky.

Flora walked alongside. "Alf, can I say something?"

"I know what you're going to say, but spit it out anyway," he said staring straight ahead.

"It's just that recently you've become distant. We used to have fun," she said, visibly let down.

"It's nowt to do with you Flora. It's just that I woke up the other day and felt soddin' miserable, right through to my marrow. Haven't been able to shake it off. Since I've been getting out in this chair, it's revived memories of what it was like before. I used to be so soddin' active, and on top of that..." He paused to choose his words carefully: "I've a feeling that our Roland is up to no good. I haven't got to the bottom of it yet, but I'm getting closer. Point is... if I'm right... what then?"

"For a minute I thought you'd gone off me," said Flora with relief.

They arrived at the viewpoint at the top or the hill, and then faced the vista of the rolling hills above the village.

"We haven't played our game for ages. Don't you think about me any more?" she probed.

Again he paused and thought carefully: "It's not that I don't think about you. It's just that I wouldn't know what to do if, you know, the occasion arose."

She knelt, gripped his leg, and looked him in the eye: "You just leave all that to me. Fancy a brew?"

They held on to the plastic cups of hot tea supplied by the vendor in the lay-by. As they surveyed the view, Sir Alf's eyes began to fill, but not through the chill of the breeze.

Contemplation at Bullock Units

Roland sat in his swivel chair and pondered his next move. The antics of the Jakeson brothers had scared him. A cold sweat had enveloped him when he found out about the poisoning. Since then his imagination had run riot with alibis and explanations. He had the words typed in his mind like the script of a play, how he would disown the plot, and would not hesitate from framing Joe and the Jakeson brothers.

Seconds later, the voice of his secretary invaded his thoughts.

"Mr Bullock, a call for you."

He picked up the receiver. It was Joe. There was a nervous tremor in his voice.

"We need to talk," he said.

"How about a pie and a pint?" Roland responded, pretending not to notice his distress.

They met in the pub, ordered a meal and were sitting in silence, each mulling over his concerns. Roland, unable to stand it any longer, broke the ice.

"They think it was revenge. They'll never suspect us of having anything to do with the poisoning," he smiled. "Couldn't have been better if we'd planned it."

Unfortunately, Joe didn't see this as a bonus: "Poisoning! I don't remember agreeing to… poisoning!!" he hissed.

They both looked round to see if anyone had heard.

"Me neither, but we appear to have got away with it," Roland replied smugly.

Joe wasn't convinced: "I can't sleep proper for thinking what might have happened. I keep seeing myself in nick, explaining that we only meant to stop the game, but ended up wiping out the whole soddin' team."

"Calm down, for God's sake," said Roland, getting concerned that he would give the game away.

The meal arrived and Roland tucked in. Joe picked up the knife and fork, and stared at the utensils as they danced in his hands. They clattered on the table as he lost control.

"Get a grip," Roland sputtered through a mouth full of pie and chips.

Joe picked at his meal. Then, unable to continue, he rested the knife and fork across his plate. It was an unfortunate choice of words from the waitress that set him off again.

"Is everything all right?" she innocently enquired.

"No, everything is not bloody well all right!" he barked.

Roland intervened: "Sorry love, the food's fine. Don't bother about my friend here, he's just had a bad day."

The waitress scurried away carrying the used dishes. Minutes later, she nervously returned clutching a mini spiral-bound pad and a stubby pencil.

"Would you like dessert?" she croaked.

A remorseful Joe thanked her for the thought and instead opted for the solace of the bar's top shelf. It was at this point that Roland started having doubts about their partnership. He began to view Joe as more of a puppet, someone to be used and manipulated, someone to do his dirty business.

"Let me get you another," he said viewing the gesture as an investment.

After two more off the top shelf, Joe became more relaxed. 'Pliable,' Roland thought.

"Now what are we going to do about this weekend's fixture?"

"Better ask the Jakesons. They seem to have it all in hand."

Joe downed his tot in one and grimaced as the rough alcohol bit the back of his throat.

Roland's tone changed to that of restrained irritation: "They're your men, you engaged them. You find out what they've got planned." He turned to the chap behind the bar. "Bill please."

He turned back to Joe. "I'll give you a ring tomorrow. Have some answers." Then he leaned closer and whispered with a hint of menace. "Bit of advice, don't get pissed and mouth off!"

Joe nodded without making eye contact.

The afternoon turned into early evening and the pub had filled up considerably by the time Joe came to leave. As he stepped off his bar stool, he had to keep hold of the bar rail for support. He eyed the doorway and set off. 'A fortuitous circumstance,' he thought, as he used the other customers for support as he made his way out.

The cool fresh air hit him in the face. He only just made it into the car park where he retched up the consumption of the past two hours. He staggered to the shop where his secretary aided him into his office and sat him in his chair.

"What on earth...?"

She was about to ask what he had been up to, but the stench of his breath put her in the picture.

"Ha, ha, self-inflicted, and this early in the week. Well, you'll get no sympathy from me," she said.

Not wanting to listen to a girl half his age talk to him like she was his mother he retaliated.

"Just get me coffee and pills, or piss off and don't come back."

Half an hour later, he ventured out to see where the coffee was. His day was made complete when he cast his glazed eyes around the office. No coffee, no secretary or her belongings ~ just a manila envelope on her chair addressed to him. He didn't open it. Instead he turned the door sign to *Closed* and locked it. Returning to his office he muttered: "Shit, shit, shit."

Hard Work Rewarded at The Flyer

"The share holders would like to show their appreciation of your endeavours in raising sales by ten percent. They're all very pleased," said the regional manager as he held out an envelope.
Arnold Boswell showed no restraint as he eagerly ripped it open. "Thank you," he beamed as he waved the cheque for five hundred pounds.
"Keep this up and there'll be another next month," added the manager.

No Reward for Geoffrey

He arrived home after a notably unsuccessful day to find the house empty. He had hoped for loving care and sympathy, but his heart sank as the realisation of gloom dawned.

"Just great! Not a soul. No welcome home for the breadwinner. No food, no sod all. Well, bugger this."

He dumped his brief case in the hall and banged the front door behind him. Marching down the drive, he heard his name being whispered.

"Psst. Over here."

Geoffrey turned to see Albert lurking in the corner of his garage.

"Come here," he beckoned, crooking his finger.

Geoffrey's rumbling stomach always dominated his mood, and he was just about to die of hunger.

"A bit over the top this. What the hell's up?" he said as they stood in the gloom of the unlit garage.

"It's about the game on Sunday. It's a Cup match, are you still on?"

"Still on what?"

"Don't mess me about. You know what I'm on about," replied Albert.

"Yes all right, so long as we don't kill anyone," said Geoffrey.

"Now look, we've got to make sure the other side wins, though just at this moment I'm not sure how," puzzled Albert.

"Simple, bribe the umpire."

Albert smiled, and then added: "There's two of them. Can't just bribe one, it'll have to be both."

"What's it worth, a crate of ale?" enquired Geoffrey innocently.

"You're joking. Their reputations are on the line here, at least two… each."

Geoffrey's eyes scanned the garage. "Frig! How am I going to get four crates of ale?"

"You work there don't you?" Albert said slyly. "The team doesn't have to lose by a mile, perhaps just a technicality…"

Momentarily, as a shaft of streetlight highlighted the furrows on his neighbour's face, Geoffrey thought he saw the devil.

"Ok, I'll sort out the beer. You sort the umpires," he said.

"Deal," said Albert.

"Cobblers to the cricket," they whispered as they shook hands.

They both peered out from the corner of the garage. Seeing that the coast was clear, Albert dashed inside and Geoffrey tiptoed back towards his home. As he reached the road, he noticed that the light was now on in his lounge.

"Sod it," he mumbled. "I'm off for a pint."

As he got out of earshot of the houses, he muttered, "Technicality'. I like that, what a good man."

Two hours later and mellowing nicely, he entered the front door of his house. This time, all the lights were on and a rich aroma of cooked chicken persuaded his already beer-enhanced taste buds that he could manage a portion or two.

"Smells good," he announced to the empty hallway.

A surprisingly reassuring reply came from the kitchen.

"Sorry I wasn't here when you arrived home. I thought you might've gone to the pub," Susan called.

Geoffrey looked confused.

"Your case was in the hallway."

"Curious thing," Susan remarked, between mouthfuls, as they ate off their knees whilst watching TV.

"What is?" said Geoffrey not taking his eyes away from the screen.

"As I pulled up the drive, I could have sworn I saw two men huddled in next door's garage... in the dark."

"Nowt to do with me!!" Geoffrey almost choked on a spud.

"I didn't say it was."

"Anyway, you haven't told me why you were so late," he said, hastily trying to change the subject.

"Another emergency meeting at the cricket club. You wouldn't believe all the work involved. We have to win the game on Sunday, you know."

"Really," he replied trying not to show interest. "Is everyone well enough now?"

"All, apart from the pro. He's not fit yet."

"Shame," said Geoffrey with the wrong accent on his voice.

Another Game Underway

Geoffrey arrived home mid-afternoon and, as usual, on home game fixtures. He had to weave through the cars parked down the street. Deep inside, he was bursting to know what plot Albert had engineered in order to halt the play. He decided to play his own waiting game.

"Mustn't give anything away. Ignore the temptation to ask: 'Have you enjoyed yourself? How's the game gone?' Just let it pour out. Whatever happens, don't show any interest at all." He looked at his watch. "Bloody hell, another two hours. How on earth can I fill the time?" He smiled as he opened the fridge. As he reached in, his smile widened. "Better have a beer. Just like the ones the umpires will have later."

Albert was also on tenterhooks. He was in the driveway waxing the car's every detail to prolong the operation, but secretly listening for any hint of an uproar. It was then he noticed a mini-coach cruising up and down. Not thinking it was anything of consequence, he responded positively to his wife's continuous demand for him to go and get his tea. Halfway through his ham salad, with a mouth full of boiled egg, it happened. The cheers and commotion that erupted from the ground could be heard for miles.

"Yes!" he shouted, as if he had just scored a Cup Final goal, and in the process showered his wife in part-chewed boiled egg.

Geoffrey also heard the cheer and celebrated the, as yet unqualified, victory of the plot with another beer.

During the past hour he had not been entirely idle. He had practised in the mirror various methods of consolation. "Don't worry love, there'll be another year," was the first he threw out on the basis of untruth. "At least we'll be able to sell our house," seemed a bit crass and, "You'll be able to meet some nice new neighbours," had him in stitches. So instead he decided to play dumb. "Say nowt," he said, mimicking a local accent. Unfortunately his rehearsals had not prepared him for the events of an hour later.

Reclining in his usual recumbent position on the settee, and surrounded by empty bottles, he was brought back to reality by the unceremonious entrance of his wife and daughter. Clutching the freezer box, and with a mixture of anger and grief, they clattered their way into the kitchen. The noise of the freezer box being thrown in a corner was immediately upstaged by the sound of Susan ranting.

"Somebody up there doesn't want us to win. Somebody round here doesn't want us to win!"

Alison just stood there and wailed. Hearing all the commotion, Geoffrey paused for a moment. His thoughts raced as best they could in the fog of Old Goat Ale. 'Obviously not gone their way,' he mused. 'Now then, what we have here is a rather delicate situation. Not exactly my style, I grant you, but bucket loads of tact required.' He gave it a minute, accurately timed by the clock on the video, then hands in pockets and sporting an exaggerated gait he strolled into the kitchen.

Ignoring the obvious, he enquired: "What's up love?"

Alison had red eyes and Susan's face was streaked with tears.

Almost unintelligibly Susan explained: "Game abandoned... girls... babies on pitch... no captain... bat too big... ball too big."

Geoffrey didn't pretend to understand: when in doubt, make a brew.

"You can tell me all about it over a cup of tea," he said.

He turned away quickly to hide a smirk that was creeping to the corners of his mouth. 'Don't smile for God's sake,' flashed through his mind as he filled the kettle. He turned round, but they were busy hanging up their coats. As the water boiled, he just looked on. Then Susan stared back and caught him correcting a guilty grin.

"If I thought you had something to do with this!" she said accusingly.

He stirred the contents of the cups. Then he held out the cups of tea.

"Charming! I'm sitting here guarding the fort, then get accused of doing something I'm not remotely interested in."

Susan softened: "I'm sorry. It's just that every time we get an opportunity to save the club, something happens to wreck it."

"So what's happened this time?" asked Geoffrey, keen to find out.

Susan blew her nose, took a deep breath, and explained: "They batted first. We bowled them out for 170, an easy score to reach. Everybody's excited that a win is on its way. Then the substitute pro comes in, and within five minutes these six girls walk on to the pitch holding babies. As they walk on, they're chanting: 'Your baby!! Your baby!! What you going to do?'"

Geoffrey's face changed to that of mystified shock.

"He'd only been married a week and his wife was in the seats. She ran out of the ground and he went after her and the girls followed. While all this is going on, one umpire measures the bat and ball with his callipers, and the other gets out his tape in the out field. Then they have a chat and the game's abandoned. We've been accused of cheating and declared losers pending an investigation."

Geoffrey could hardly contain his admiration for Albert's efforts.

"That's awful," he sympathised.

On the basis that he might give the game away, he changed the subject. "Biscuit?" he offered, as he held a pack of digestives towards his daughter.

Joe Lagg Employs a New Secretary

Since his drunken afternoon and the unceremonious departure of his secretary, Joe Lagg had been finding out just how complicated his own office was and how useless he was at running it. His effort at independence came crashing down at his first attempt. He couldn't even start the computer, let alone construct a business letter. He even managed to scald the back of his hand while attempting to fill the coffee maker after it had boiled dry. Sitting in his office, sipping muddy coffee and cradling his bandaged hand, he thought it could get no worse.

An instantly recognisable voice echoing from the front of the shop indicated otherwise. "Hello!" shouted Susan Perkins.

Joe decided to lay low and hope that she would disappear.

"Hello!" she repeated.

Joe sat motionless for a few minutes and presumed she had gone. Then the door opened abruptly. Susan, framed by the white architrave and silhouetted by the bright sunlight, appeared to Joe like the angel of death.

"No, I'm not ready to go yet!" he screamed.

He recoiled foetal-like to the back of his chair. The sudden movement jolted his cup, resulting in muddy coffee once again being directed by his newspaper into his lap. He stared at her as the warm liquid reached his skin.

"I have no answers for you. I don't know anything. Leave me alone!" he shouted pressing himself towards the back of his chair.

"Calm down," she said advancing towards him with a paper towel. "This is becoming a habit with you," she smiled as she mopped his desk.

"Don't touch me!" shouted Joe defending his head with his bandaged hand.

"I'm not going to harm you. I'm here to help you," she soothed.

"Let's start by cleaning you up. Then you can sign my contract of employment."

A twitch that had started in Joe's eye on the afternoon he got drunk developed into a full facial movement.

"Ffffrigging joking if you think I'm taking yyyyou on," he stammered.

"Let's put our cards on the table," she oozed, making herself comfortable in the chair opposite.

He looked down, unaware she was speaking metaphorically.

"How many others have applied?" Susan was confident that no one else would have applied for the job.

Joe looked up. "Well none, actually. But I put a big ad in the local paper…"

Susan rose from the chair, put her hands on her hips and leaned slightly forward.

"The lady you sacked is very bitter. She's telling everyone she meets what a shit employer you are. To quote her words, you're a 'bullying, hard faced, chauvinistic bastard'… Coffee?"

She left the room and he relaxed his position. Catching his own reflection in a picture on his desk, he noticed his face twitching. He put his hand there to stop it, but it continued. He pondered the coffee-stained crossword and tried to focus. But the clues took on a strange angle, and then began to rotate faster and faster. He rubbed his eyes but it did not help, then the room began to spin. He gripped the sides of the chair, took a deep breath and it began to slow down. Sweat dripped from his brow.

"I feel awful sick," he moaned. Head in his hands, he tried to rationalise recent events. "One minute, everything's fine. The next, business is crap, I'm branded a lousy employer, and it's more luck than good judgement that I'm not banged up for murder."

A voice that he didn't recognise suggested: "Coffee? Fresh, strong, coffee?"

The angel of death had changed to the angel of mercy. She moved the papers and placed a steaming cafetiere in front of him. He smiled as though he had been rescued from a terrible fate. He watched her fingers grip the round top of the plunger, then slowly depress it till it touched the lid.

She stood and watched as he drooled over the fresh Colombian. He closed his eyes and breathed in the aroma. Then he looked up with a puzzled expression. "Mrs Perkins, can I…"

"Susan," she interjected.

"Susan… I'm not well at the moment, as you can see. I need a break, lot on my mind. I was thinking of closing the shop for a while. Could you come back next week?"

Susan sat on the edge of his desk.

"I have a better idea. You take a few days off and leave the keys. I'll open up for you and make a note of all the happenings. It's not good for business to close up… all those missed opportunities."

He smiled thinly in acknowledgment.

"How come you want to work here? I thought you hated me."

"I do hate you," she replied in an inoffensive voice. "But you need a secretary, and I need a job."

"Oh," he replied, slightly taken aback.

"Geoffrey's job isn't as secure as we thought. Beer sales have dropped since the poisoning. Happy now?"

He looked up at the ceiling, nodding. He saw the logic of the arrangement, but felt he was being manipulated. Yet he also felt as though he could trust her. This worried him too. But as he rose and held out the keys, he felt a great weight lift from his shoulders. He walked from the shop as though he was leaving forever.

"How on earth did you manage that?" said Geoffrey to Susan over the evening meal.

"Easy," she quipped.

"Mind you, I'd heard that he's cracking up. That pissed the other night, he fell off his stool."

Susan pushed away her meal and stood up: "You always belittle the things I do."

"Susan, I didn't..."

But his words of explanation were never received.

"Up you!" she said.

First Day, New Job

The following day, Susan unlocked the front door of the shop, switched on the lights and put on the kettle. Looking round, she spotted a pile of unopened letters against the wall where the door had swept them. Previously she had been wondering how to fill the day. Now she knew.

Despair Sets In

The season moved speedily on. For the committee at the cricket club, the prospects of survival were looking increasingly slim.

"After all we've done," said John Appleby with a sigh. "Fat chance of winning the league. It's all over. No pro will come here, chance they get poisoned." He slumped in his chair.

The committee members stared at one another across the table, each looking for stimulus, but none was forthcoming.

Arthur looked across at Tom and grinned: "What we need is some lubrication for the wheels of inspiration."

"Aye, for God's sake, more like a bloody wake," said Tom rising from his seat.

The rest looked on as they approached the bar. Tom raised the shutters and switched on the bar lights. As the fluorescent bulb flashed into life, he offered a diversion.

"What we have here is the latest offering from Old Goat Brewery. They've kindly donated a barrel free of charge for us to sample and give our opinion." Tom tapped the pump with his index finger.

"On account of they can't sell it," added Arthur. "Apparently sales aren't what they should be." Arthur lined up the beers. "Pints for men, halves for ladies… it's only fair."

The problems of the club diminished as they quaffed the ale. Then they each gave their own verdict and the probable punter reaction.

Fred Pickup's turn came first. Imitating a connoisseur, he held it to the light, rinsed it round the glass, took a swig and pronounced:

"We really need to observe the problem from a different angle."

The others tilted their glasses and stared into the clear liquid.

"No, not the beer ~ the problem, here, in this club. You see, we've been trying to solve the wrong problem."

Arthur and Tom raised their glasses.

"Works every time. Let me top you up," said Arthur.

"Go on Fred," said Janice eager to hear what he had to say.

"You see, we've been trying to get cash for Benjamin and trying to win a Cup to save the club. Really we should be letting Benjamin generate his own money. Then we can concentrate on fixing it so that it doesn't matter if we don't get a Cup."

"Brilliant, what a man!" said Janice grinning from ear to ear.

"Fine, but how does he generate his own money?" said John, not entirely convinced.

"He can organise the Rasta night, he's always going on about it," said Susan.

"Frigg's a Rasta night?" Tom whispered into Arthur's ear.

"Not a clue, but it sounds Italian," Arthur answered.

Fred swilled the beer around again before taking a swig, swallowed, then smiled in acknowledgement.

"The problem of the Cup is that it's impossible for us to win one now. So somehow we have to change this ten year rule."

John Appleby put down his glass. "Before we go much further, I'd like to clarify a point" The others stared in silence. "This business with the Cup, it's nowt to do with Alf Bullock. In fact he sympathises with us. It's his son, Roland."

"They're all peeing in the same bucket as far as I'm concerned," said Tom Deakin accusingly.

"No it's right," confirmed Fred. "After all it was him who lent us the two grand."

"Leave this Cup business to me," said Susan softly.

They looked in her direction out of common courtesy, but little credence was given.

Tom continued to address the others. "Another thing... is it me, or do these happenings, poisoning and things, seem more than just accidental occurrences. All them babies... Crikey, someone's putting 'em up to it."

"Aye, and there's only one man that'll profit from us not winning owt ~ frigging Roland Bullock," added John with venom.

The others nodded, but did not add to his statement. Janice turned to Susan: "So how do you plan to...?"

Susan stopped her in mid-sentence.

"Just leave it to me," she replied confidently. Truth was she hadn't a clue.

"Another half please, Arthur," she added holding out her glass to change the subject. "What's it called?" she inquired.

Arthur spluttered it out through fits of laughter. "Old Plodder's Piddle. A Commemorative ale to mourn the passing of 'Neddy' at Hillside Farm."

"What's so funny?" asked Janice.

Susan just shrugged her shoulders.

Later That Evening

Geoffrey had retired for the night and was snoring loudly by the time Susan arrived home. Awakened by the bedroom light being switched on, he half-inquired: "Good meeting?"
Sitting on the edge of the bed, she turned away, sneered, and continued rolling down her tights.
"All this time and I never twigged someone was sabotaging the game," she added in hushed terms.
Geoffrey who had started to drift away suddenly became all ears.
"What… no… who?" he stuttered.
"Can't mention names till we're hundred per cent sure. But we're ninety nine per cent there already."
Aided by the beer, Susan fell into a deep slumber as soon as her head hit the pillow. Geoffrey, on the other hand didn't sleep at all.

The Second Day of the New Job

Susan arrived at her office to find the light flashing on the answer phone. She ignored it till she had made a coffee, then pad and pen at the ready, pressed the playback.

"Susan… Joe here. I've decided I'm going to be off at least a fortnight. I feel like crap. Any problems, use your initiative. Don't call me…"

"Cheeky bastard," she shouted at the machine.

Same Day Up at the Bullock House

Sir Alf was tidying up after making his own breakfast. He was stretching towards the shelf to replace the cups, when he heard a voice behind him.

"Let me do that."

"Flora, I've missed you," he said, more sincerely than he ever thought possible.

Without any hesitation, she hugged him like a long-lost friend.

"Coffee, then I'll tell you all about it," she gushed.

They sat opposite one another at the kitchen table. Although they had previously felt like just good friends, to his surprise they automatically held hands across the table. Flora told him about the aromatherapy course she had been on for the past three weeks.

"It was brilliant, all the wonderful effects, cures and feelings that you can imagine."

"What, from just a smell?" he said trying not to be negative.

"It's more than just a smell. The oils are taken in by the skin. It affects the whole body, mind and spirit."

"Curious," he said not entirely convinced. "When I used to get oil on my hands, we were told to wash it off cos it'd do you harm."

"That was engine oil, this is essential oil," she replied confidently.

"Engine oil is essential too, you know," he teased.

"Ah, engine oil. Good for the engine, bad for you," added Flora trying to put it in simple terms. "Still no news from your wife then?" she asked looking round.

"She's gone," he replied bluntly.

"Gone where?"

"Don't rightly know. She just left a note saying she's going to get some sun," he sniped.

"On your own then. Are you coping?"

"Coping's a good way to describe it. Yes."

"How's the legs?" she said grabbing his knee.

"I thought I felt something the other day ~ you know, a tingle, a shudder."

"Nothing since?" she asked.

"No," he said dolefully.

"I'll clean up, then we'll have another brew."

"Ok," he said forcing a smile.

During her clean up, Flora investigated the room she had spotted before she went away. 'Ideal,' she enthused as she closed the door behind her.

119

Over their next tea break, Flora encouraged Sir Alf to go and get some fresh air.

"It's a brilliant day and I'll need more time to get this place sorted. You might as well."

"You sure? Looks bloody cold to me" he protested.

"Get wrapped up, you'll be ok," she replied not taking no for an answer. She smiled and looked him in the eyes as she fastened his seatbelt a little too tight for his comfort.

"Go easy, you'll cut me bloody circulation off," he remarked as a grin cracked across his face.

He whizzed the wheelchair out on to the lane and up towards the viewpoint. As the breeze flicked his hair, he began to unwind. He stopped between a line of parked cars. He took a few deep breaths of fresh air and sighed.

"Is life complicated… or what?" He looked to either side. 'Can't understand it,' he thought. 'Like a row of bloody fish tanks.'

Inside the cars, the occupants stared through the misted-up windows, the steam billowing from their opened flasks.

"All this way to sit in your car" he muttered under his breath

Alongside him, one such occupant wiped the window and condensation ran down the glass. A solemn face peered out.

"Get some fresh air, you'll feel much better," he mouthed. He looked back across the rolling landscape. 'She were bloody right,' he thought, as Flora's words echoed in his head.

On his way back up the drive, he became aware of a change. Something different, but he didn't figure it out till he got closer.

"Curtains closed in the middle of the day?"

He got to the front door and a faint flowery smell made him sniff the air like a bloodhound.

"What the hell's she using as polish?"

A bigger shock was to greet him as he opened the door.

"Jesus, what have you done?" he said to Flora, who was standing in the hallway in a white smock.

As he peered into the semi-darkness he spotted candles flickering in tiny pots all the way across the landing on the next floor. He looked up and cocked an ear to the faint relaxation music drifting from above. A curious grin emerged on his face.

"What the?"

"Nothing for you to worry about. Just relax and do as you're told," she said trying to keep a straight face.

"I'm not worried, more… baffled."

They made their way up in the lift and followed the scent of the candles towards the music. She pushed open the door and eased him beyond the threshold. His face was a picture.

The room was lit entirely by night-light candles places on every surface and all apparently dancing to the rhythm of the relaxation tape. White drapes had been simply, but effectively, stapled to the walls and ceiling. In the centre of the room, a single bed was covered in white towels.

"Bloody hell, who's being sacrificed?" he gasped.

"You are, if you don't shut up!" she teased.

She wheeled him in and parked him alongside the bed. She cleared her throat, even though she did not need to.

"There's no other way to put this, so take your pants down and lie on the bed."

"That course has done wonders for your brass neck, I'll say that," he said, startled at her bluntness. "Shrinking violet when you went away."

"Just do as you're told… not had a massage before, have you?"

"Never had nowt like this."

He thought it best to comply, so he slid onto the bed. After undoing his laces, he let his shoes drop to the floor.

"The belt buckle and fly," she insisted pointing to his waist.

"I know where it is," he replied, getting shirty.

The moment he had undone his zipper, she grabbed his turn-ups and without hesitation pulled off his pants.

"Hey up!" he shouted, startled at the swiftness of his de-bagging.

"Just relax and enjoy," she said while mixing the aromatic oils in a small white dish.

"It'll be difficult, but I'll try," he said mischievously.

As the massage progressed, he found that the enjoyment was being marred by the lack of control of a certain part of his anatomy. The part, unaffected by the paralysis, was indeed responding to the treatment and about to provide him with some embarrassment.

"Go easy Flora, you're winding me up."

He started coughing in an attempt to cool things off.

"That's the whole idea. Got to get the blood surging to places it's not been to for a while. Relax," she reassured him.

"Well you're certainly doing that. It's just that, you know…"

Flora followed his eyes, although she knew quite well what he was referring to.

"Oh that, you'll have to do better than that," she added in a much softer, lower, tone.

She applied more hot oil to the palms of her hands then massaged the full length of his legs.

121

"Bloody hell, Flora," he oozed.

An hour or so later, he was awakened by Flora standing at his side.

"So how do you feel?" she asked softly.

He was wrapped in towelling from head to foot. "This has to be heaven," he enthused. "Wonderful. I've not felt like this since... come to think of it I've never felt like this before." Then he added in a hushed tone, "Flora, that was brilliant."

"And we got a result," she beamed.

He looked puzzled.

"Your legs! They weren't exactly thrashing about, more pulsing and twitching... Coffee's there when you're ready," she stroked her hand down his legs as she left. "No hurry," she added as she closed the door.

The Plot Thickens

Susan sat at her desk pondering her next move. Having promised to sort out Roland, she was now confronted with 'how?' 'Me and my big mouth,' she thought. Her head swam with plots and theories, but nothing seemed plausible. 'Seemed to have it all worked out last night. Just dig some dirt, then throw it at him, blackmail, easy.'
Staring through the window, she spotted a forlorn canvasser harassing passers-by.
"Eu-bloody-reka," she said somewhat louder than she intended.
A young mum, carrying her baby, and perusing the *For Sale* boards twitched her nose and grimaced. She shoved her hand down the side of her baby's nappy, tilted her head sideways and mouthed, "Jesus."
"Everything ok?" said Susan.
"Yes, but it's an awful mess down here."
After lunch, Susan locked the front door and turned the sign to indicate that the shop was closed. To complete the ruse, she switched off the display lights. Sitting at the desk in the back office, she went through her notes again then dialled the number for Bullock Units.
"Is Roland, err... Mr. Bullock in?"
"Who's calling?" The secretary was eating her lunch. It sounded as if her mouth was half-filled with sandwich.
Susan's original idea was to remain anonymous, but she hadn't thought of a name. She frantically searched for inspiration. There were only two books on Joe Lagg's desk, a dictionary and a thesaurus.
"It's Miss Rogets from The Throttle Flyer," she stuttered.
Susan heard the message being passed on.
"Mr Bullock, there's a lady on the phone. A journalist with a French name."
Susan heard the connection click and gripped her notes.
"Miss Rogets, what can I do for you?" he said smarmily.
"We're doing a feature on local people in charge of industry ~ people who are forging a name for themselves as leaders. We wondered if you, as a local entrepreneur, would like to give a comment."
There was a pause and a loud farting noise as Roland sat up in his chair. Susan heard the noise and shook the phone. "Mr. Bullock... are you there?"
"Well, I'm flattered," he choked.
"I'll need to take some background details first," she said getting the hang of it.
'Recognition had to come eventually,' he thought to himself, smugly.

"Can we start with your history and education," she interrupted. Susan made notes furiously as he prattled on. After what seemed like an age, she managed to stop what had developed into a monologue. "Thank you Mr. Bullock, that'll be fine."

"Do you need any pictures... when will it be published?" he excitedly asked.

"Err, Soon. Better go now," Susan replaced the receiver and blew an exaggerated sigh of relief.

Roland was left with the receiver to his ear, as it clicked then buzzed. His face remained motionless as he pondered the amateurish finality to the call. His eyes screwed up as the euphoria quickly turned to suspicion. He shouted through to his secretary:

"Get me The Throttle Flyer will you!"

Within seconds, Roland's feelings had raced through a list of emotions: excitement, suspicion, disappointment and finally humiliation.

"So you don't have a Miss Roget's then? You're not doing a piece on local business personalities?"

The journalist on the other end burst into laughter.

"I get the message," he held the phone slightly above its rest and let it drop. "Bastard," he added to the clatter.

Back in the office, Susan was using Directory Enquiries to get numbers to fit the names Roland had divulged. She finally thought she was getting somewhere.

"We're planning a party for a former classmate of yours, a Roland Bullock, and we wished to surprise him with a few facts he may have forgotten about... I wonder if you could help?"

"I don't know about being a mate, but I can certainly tell you a thing or two about him," said a gruff voice.

"Sounds promising. Do you mind if we meet?"

They met the following day at a pub in the nearby village of Ashwert. Jack, a haulier's son, recalled the cold traumatic experiences of public school education with Roland. After talking to Jack for a while, she got the impression he wasn't on Roland's Christmas card list.

"So you're not exactly an old chum then?"

"No, he turned out to be a right twat."

Susan thought it best to come clean. She told him of her plan and was surprised by his response.

"Why didn't you say earlier?" he enthused. "If it's proper dirt you want ~ names, places and times ~ I think we can sort you out. Cost you a pint though."

She hurried to the bar as Jack cast his mind back to the days of cold showers and corporal punishment.

Later the Same Day

Geoffrey arrived home from work and spotted Albert in his garage.
"Albert... Glad I've caught you."
Albert was painting a plastic tub to make it look like a half-barrel, a painful, sacrilegious exercise that up to two years ago he would never have contemplated.
"What?" he shouted objecting to the interruption.
"They know it's you, up at the club. They know what you've been up to."
"I haven't been up to anything," said Albert getting vexed.
"Poisoning, bribery, and all," Geoffrey stuttered. "And corruption... in my book that's getting up to a hell of a lot."
"I had nowt to do with poisoning. Bribery maybe," Albert paused then grinned. "But you're in it too, right up to your neck. If I go down, I'll take you with me."
"Ok, ok, keep your hair on," said Geoffrey nervously twitching.
The realisation that he too could be implicated had him pacing back and forth in the garage.
"Is there anything they can pin on us?" he asked anxiously.
"Not unless the umpires split on us ~ but that incriminates them as well."
"So what was Susan on about last night? She said they knew who it was."
"Maybe she's fishing, trying to trip you up? You must've said something in your sleep, or more like when you've been pissed. You must be pissed every night ~ dustmen complain like hell about carrying away your empties."
"Nowt to do with you. My drinking habits are my business, I'll have you know it's me that's keeping the firm going."
"Going bust from what I hear," snapped Albert, a laugh mixing in with his words.
Geoffrey faced him nose to nose. "You're a snidey bastard at heart, aren't you?"
Albert looked at the ground: "I didn't mean it. It just comes out."
"I'll do some asking round, see what I can come up with," said Geoffrey, setting off home.
"Drop us in it and you want stuffing!" cussed Albert.
"Have some faith," were Geoffrey's final words.
"Last bloke who had faith got crucified," muttered Albert.
He returned to his painting.

Tentative Inquiries During Breakfast

"You know the other night," said Geoffrey, doing his best, but giving an unconvincing impersonation of someone who wasn't bothered about the reply.

"Yes," said Susan.

"Did I hear you say that you knew who was responsible for the poisoning… and things?"

"You did," she replied giving nothing away.

"So who is it then?" he asked outright as his curiosity got the better of him.

"What's it to you?"

"Just being nosy." Seeing he was getting nowhere, he decided on a different tack. "Our beer sales have slumped since the poisoning."

"But you've been cleared!"

"Ah, but folk are queer like that. No smoke without fire..."

"Get Alison to school or she'll be late. We'll continue this later."

Geoffrey, somewhat unwilling, did as he was bid.

As soon as they had gone, Susan got out her notepad. "Responsible for poisoning and bankrupting the brewery," she said as she wrote.

Later that day, she phoned Roland.

"Bullock Units, can I help?" said the robotic voice of the secretary.

"Hello, it's Mrs Rogets from The Flyer. Is Mr Bullock in?"

The secretary immediately put her hand over the receiver and whispered loudly: "It's that woman from The Flyer."

"Put her on," said Roland preparing himself. He sat upright in his chair and picked up the receiver. "Mrs Rogets, didn't expect to hear from you so soon," he said not giving anything away.

"Mr Bullock, something's cropped up, we're doing another feature about the impending demise of the local cricket club and we wondered if you'd like to comment?"

Silence from Roland.

"Shall I take that as 'no comment'? Well, we're doing another feature on schoolboys who've slept with their tutors. Would you like to comment on that then? Are you still there Mr Bullock, or should I call you Master Bollock?"

Roland let the receiver drop on to the rest. Sitting back in his chair, he could feel sweat dampening his shirt.

"What a nasty piece of goods," he murmured.

"Something wrong?" said the secretary poking her head round the door.

"I think one of my skeletons slipped out for a walk."

She didn't reply, just twisted her face in puzzlement.

Susan sat with the phone buzzing at her ear for a moment, and then replaced it to its rest. 'How would he react? He wouldn't just change the ten year rule. That'd be too easy. He would lose face. Violence perhaps?' She pondered about his state of mind.

Moments later, she found out. The phone rang. She stared at it uneasily, her hand poised above, and then the machine clicked in. After the recorded message, she froze as she heard Roland's voice.

"Meet me at The Ram Inn at seven. Bring the brothers. We have a problem to solve."

He didn't notice the lady sitting at a nearby table when he arrived at the pub. If he had looked closer, he would have noticed she was wearing a hat, scarf and overcoat even though it was a summer's evening. He ordered a drink, then sat for ten minutes. When he looked at his watch, the niggle was written on his face. He reached into his pocket for his phone. This time, he dialled Joe Lagg's mobile number.

"Hell are you?" he hissed.

"In bed, off sick. Flu or sommat. Where are you?" he said nasally.

"I'm in the pub waiting for you. Don't you listen to your answer phone?"

"I've told you, I'm off sick," he said weakly.

"Sick or not, we have to talk ~ urgently. I'm not prepared to go over it on the phone."

As he spoke, he noticed an over-dressed lady near the window and focused on her.

"Tomorrow. Fine. In here then. The brothers too, don't forget."

When he turned back she had gone, leaving her drink untouched.

"Who's the woman in the window seat?" he asked the barman.

"Never seen her before."

Roland tilted his head. "Another whiskey please... hell of a day."

The same sentiment was going through Susan's mind as she left.

"Just a wincey bit too close for comfort," she said to the pavement as she kept her head down.

Next day, she decided to take a rest. 'No espionage, no lying phone calls, just a normal working day like everyone else,' she thought. A phone-call, mid morning, from the local planning officer cut short her 'normal day'.

"Is Mr Lagg in?" he asked.

"He's off sick. He's left me in charge. Can I help?"

"Probably not. There are a few queries about the outline planning permission for the houses going on the old cricket ground," he said casually.

"The cricket ground?" she repeated.

"Yes, you must know it. Throttle Cricket Club just up the road from you."

"Of course, I know where it is," she said getting agitated.

"Apparently it's not being used any more," he added coolly.

"Of course it's bloody used. There's a game on this weekend," Susan shouted.

She hung up the phone. Then, she ushered the browsing customers out of the shop.

"Sorry, it's an emergency, we have to close."

"Don't know how you make a do," said a disgruntled gent banging the door behind him.

She closed down the shop and then sat at her desk. She went over her script, and then dialled Roland's number. Getting straight through to him, threw her off balance.

"Ah, Mrs. Rogets. I've been waiting for your call."

"Oh," she said with a tremble in her voice.

"Let's put our cards on the table. I know you don't work at The Flyer and it's unlikely that Rogets is your real name. Am I right? So what exactly are you up to?"

Susan was dumb struck. 'Bastard,' she thought.

"I haven't got all day, so if you'd like to get to the point, maybe we can come to an understanding."

She exploded: "Understanding! With you? You underhanded weasel!"

"Steady on," he replied calmly.

Irrationally, she thought it time to declare her hand.

"I'm a friend of the cricket club, the one that you intend to build on. We know that you're responsible for..."

"Ah, it's 'we' now. So there's more than one of you?" he jibed. "You can't prove a thing, so if you've got nothing more to add, I've got to go."

He pulled the receiver away from his ear, but he could still hear Susan ranting on the other end.

"I'll see to it that everyone knows about your school days and the business with the tutors, and what they used to call you if...if'

"If what?"

"If you don't cancel your plans to knock down the cricket club."

He paused, and then calmly stamped on Susan's plans: "Now look lady, whoever you are. Number one, I don't believe you'd go as far as to slander me for fear of going to court. Number two, plans are already in place to ensure that the cricket club loses its ground all in accordance with the rulebook. Ok?" He put down the phone.

Susan on the other end was stunned. She tried to remain calm, but it was impossible. 'I ought to put in his windows in at least,' she thought.

She sat, head in hands, for what seemed like ages. She couldn't be bothered with re-opening the shop, so she had another coffee and left. As she approached her house, she spotted Albert in his garage. He was painting more barrels.

"Hello Albert," she said. But either he didn't hear, or he was ignoring her. She blew into the air. 'Sod you then,' she thought and went into the house. Her mind went through various strategies, but all either implicated her immediately or seemed doomed to failure from the start. She watched from the kitchen window as Albert put his paint away, and then smiled.

The following lunchtime Roland swerved into the car park, then skidded his car to a halt when he saw the three foot high sketch of a part of male anatomy that he thought he had left behind in his school days.

"I thought you'd want me to get the police in. An ever so nice bobby came," said his secretary. "He didn't stop long though. He said he had other pillocks to chase..." she added innocently missing the policeman's little joke.

"Do you want me to be a bloody laughing stock? Phone the sodding Flyer, why don't you! Phone the police back and tell them to cancel their inquiries!"

Roland slammed the door as he headed towards his desk:

"I'll have her bleeding guts for this, Mrs Soddin' Rogets"

Minutes later, the secretary pushed open the door.

"They've got a suspect in custody. A man."

Roland put his head in his hands: "It's a woman, a woman has done this."

"The security video's a bit fuzzy," said the secretary, trying to be helpful.

"Oh never mind. If The Flyer rings, tell them 'no comment'. Have you organised a painter?"

The Local Nick

"The paint used for the graffiti, matches the one you've used on your barrels... very clever," the detective sniggered. "It's fairly common knowledge what you think of Mr Bullock and his cricket club. So why don't you just own up Mr. Bradley, and save us all some time?"

A constable previously at attention started to laugh

"Yes constable, can we share your joke?"

The constable did his best to maintain his composure as he revealed in courtroom fashion his discovery.

"Just made the connection sir, it's clearly a play on words. The graffiti on the doors and the owner of the company have, how shall we say, an unfortunate correlation."

At which point he was asked to leave for fear of lowering the tone of the proceedings.

Geoffrey arrived home early to find Mrs. Bradley in a state.

"They've taken him away," she wailed.

"Whose taken who where?"

"The police. They've taken Albert to the station."

"What for?"

"They wouldn't say, but it must be serious."

"How do you make that out?"

"A policeman put his hand on his head as was put in the car, I've seen it on the telly, they always do that to suspects."

Susan arrived home to find Geoffrey sitting at the kitchen table.

"Bloody hell," she remarked. "You look like you've seen a ghost!"

"They've arrested Albert. They took him away this morning."

The coat she had partly removed fell to the floor.

"What for?" she asked, louder than she intended.

"Don't know. Thought you'd know more about it than me. You said you know who's behind the goings on at the club."

"We do know, but it's got nothing to do with Albert."

"Oh," said Geoffrey feeling better. "So what on earth's he been arrested for?"

"How the hell do I know!" snapped Susan.

Later that evening, Geoffrey and Susan were settling down in front of the TV when a knock at the front door disturbed their 'quality leisure time'.

"I'll get it," he muttered as he went. "Albert! Come in, we've been worried about you."

Susan leapt out of her chair and entered the hallway. Albert remained in the doorway, under the light.

"Somebody's set me up," he snarled. "Last night someone *'borrowed'* my paint, and used it to paint slogans on Roland Bullock's door. And whoever it was, also *'borrowed'* my old coat and hat to do it in. Lucky for me, there was a security video. It's a poor picture, but the expert said that whoever it was, was smaller than me. They also said, how shall I put it, it looked like a woman's figure."

His eyes widened as he stared at Susan.

"Who'd do a thing like that? Must be someone with a grudge," Susan sniffed.

"Fancy a beer Albert?"

"A couple more like. Can't stand many more days like today. My whole life has been flashing by. At one point this afternoon, clear as day, I could see my photo on the front of the tabloids," he said.

The glass of beer, that had been pushed into his hand, was trembling.

Behind Freshly Painted Doors

"I'm afraid something's cropped up. We tried to contact your colleague, Mr. Lagg, but he was unavailable…"

Mr Trafford, the bank manager, was on the phone. Roland sensed trouble in his voice. He sat back in his chair. "Oh?" he said impatiently.

"On the proposal, you indicated that the land was no longer in use. But a few inquiries have indicated that this isn't the case. In fact, our sources advise us that the land may never be available for building."

"Oh?" repeated Roland, even more impatiently.

"As a lender in the locality, we have to be careful about our reputation. If we're seen to be jumping the gun on an issue like this, borrowers may vote with their feet. Lending is a cut-throat business these days, lots of competition…"

"Stop!" Roland shouted down the phone. "Are you going to put up the money or do I have to go somewhere else?"

"You'll get the same reaction wherever you go. You're free to shop around, of course."

"Stop right there!" Roland barked.

"We may be in a better position to do business, when the land is no longer used for its present purpose. Feel free to get in touch when…"

"Yes, thanks for the advice."

Roland hung up. He addressed the empty room: "In that case, we'll have to speed things up,' he muttered.

Up To No Good

Mrs Williamson looked out of the kitchen window towards the wooden shed beyond the vegetable patch. A feeble yellow light emitted from it.

"What does he get up to in there?" she wondered, without taking her hands out of the sink.

"He'll be messing with his bike," her husband replied from behind his paper.

"Well I don't like it. He spends far too long down there."

"Leave the lad alone. You should he grateful."

"Grateful? It's not natural! He's sitting there in the pitch dark," she shrieked.

"Gloom yes, but not pitch dark. Look, the lad is down there in the shed, pottering with his bike. We know where he is and, as far as we know, he's not up to mischief. Be bloody grateful for that."

"Suppose so, but I'm not keen," she said with resignation.

Unfortunately, Mr Williamson's reassurances were misplaced. For, as they sat down to watch the round of evening soaps, young master Williamson was plotting sinister retribution.

He had been simmering for some months since being dropped from the cricket team and the humiliation at the meeting in the local hall served only to heighten his desire to get even. He had ventured back to the pitch once or twice on practice sessions, but the ribbing from established players became too much. So now, most evenings he would sit in the shed by candlelight and dream of nasty happenings for John Appleby, club chairman and selector for the second team. He had come up with several plots only to bottle out on grounds that they were too scary. And, of course, since his very public shaming he would be prime suspect. But since the poisoning, he considered it to be an opportunity not to be missed.

"I might just be able to add to his suffering," he said through gritted teeth, as he stuck pins in a whittled effigy.

"Do you know what some bastard did last night?" said John Appleby.

He and Tom Deakin were sweeping the clubhouse in preparation for the forthcoming Rasta Night. Tom shook his head.

"There I was sitting down to me supper, when there was an hell of a racket on the front door. So I opened it, and this huge ball of newspaper was on fire."

"Kin' hell!" Tom sympathised.

"Scorched the bleeding door," John added.

Tom stopped his sweeping in astonishment.

"So I stamped it out with my foot, like you would."

"Aye," Tom concurred.

"And do you know what? It were a parcel of dog shit. All over me bleeding slippers, set fire to me turn-ups, then walked it all up the hall. Wife played bloody hell."

At this point Tom doubled over, hardly able to breathe for laughing.

"If I ever get my hands on the bastards, I'll wring their bleeding necks."

Tom tried to be sympathetic. But the vision of John stamping on the newspaper had him holding his aching sides, and he had to walk away.

"Hello... problem?" asked Janice.

Tom just pointed in John's direction and carried on laughing.

Game Underway

Two rather elderly and battered single-decker buses pulled up outside the ground. The occupants, mostly young men with shaved heads, heavily tattooed arms and wearing ex-army clothing, marched towards the clubhouse. At the same moment, Tom Deakin sidled up alongside an old adversary, an ex-player who was there to support the opposing team.

"How the hell are you?" he asked out of politeness.

"Fettling," said the man of few words.

"See you've brought some support."

"Nowt to do with us. Thought they were yours."

"Don't look like supporters. More like rent-a-mob on a day out."

"Mmmm," he speculated.

Tom followed them into pavilion and found them queuing at the bar.

John approached. "Have you seen the outfits? Anarchy international, if you ask me!"

"Then we better keep them happy," he said reaching for the phone:

"Hello, Tony? Look, if you want to shift some of that beer of yours, get your van loaded up and get down here quick. Two coach loads have turned up and they look like they've got a thirst on. Here for the duration."

The coach party settled themselves on the grass, and then it was a steady trek between the bar and the gents.

About four o'clock, a transit van arrived and three similarly dressed, but smarter gentlemen climbed out. They peered across the ground till they spotted their troops sitting on the grass alongside the sight-screen. They marched at double time towards them.

"Soddin' going on here?" one of them barked, as though on a parade ground.

"Following orders, Sir," said a voice from the back.

The man with the sergeant major presence leaned awkwardly forward and, in the contradiction of a loud whisper, told his troop what he thought: "This place should be a mass of devastation by now. Your orders were to infiltrate the ground, then stop the game by any means," he hissed.

"We're still on the 'infiltrate' bit," heckled one of the mob with a drunken titter to his voice.

The others laughed uncontrollably.

"Insubordination of the highest order. You'll all be on a charge," he threatened.

"Piss off," replied a voice from the centre of the group.

"Said that?" he ranted.

"Chill out! The beer's grand," came back the advice.

"He's right you know, best I've tasted for a long while," added his sidekick, who hadn't refused when handed a pint. Seconds later, the small crowd erupted.

"Jesus! Did you see that he knocked it clean out tut ground?" shouted an enthusiast.

The sergeant major tried again. "Charges, all of you, do you hear?" He was getting into full swing with his orders and threats, when he realised he had become the focus of attention of every spectator and one very irate chap in a white smock.

The umpire who had walked over to where he was standing volunteered some advice: "Sit thy down you bloody idiot, you're holding the bloody game up."

Sheepishly he sat amongst his squad.

"You're for it when we get back," he seethed.

As the day continued the group, including the drivers, mellowed happily. The combination of Old Plodder's Piddle, the hazy afternoon sun, and Janice Hinchcliffe's meat pie and peas, had removed their rent-a-mob mentality and replaced it with a more laid-back easy-going approach. Co-ordination and speech had eventually become a problem, so they just pointed at their open mouths when ready for a refill.

After the game had finished, an elected spokesman (the only one left with the power of speech) addressed John Appleby who had walked out onto the ground. He stood as best he could, fighting the strong desire to fall over. Then, after taking a deep intake of breath, he spoke as though his brain could only cope with two or three words at a time.

"Brilliant day... goosed now... no drivers... all pissed... no way home... what d'you think?"

"I think you're buggered lad," John said bluntly. "Mind you, night's only just beginning. We've a Rastafarian night starting an..."

The spokesman grinned, shuffled back to his mates, and related what he had heard.

"Buggered... beginning... boozing... a vegetarian fight... in an hour."

"Must be throwing frigging spuds at one another," replied a comrade.

The home side achieved a close fought victory. Although it no longer affected the outcome of the league, it did provide the basis for a rapturously intoxicating night. Janice went home to get changed and returned clutching the Saturday evening edition of The Throttle Flyer. She was sporting a very broad grin.

"Have you seen this?" she asked Fred gleefully.

"Famous at last!" he shouted to John, who was only just within earshot. He waved the paper in the air and tried again. "You're in the paper, a star is born," he mocked.

"Where's Tom?" he said angrily as he read the headline: Blaze hero puts foot in it.

By eight-thirty, the club was thumping to the musical beat provided by Benjamin. He had brought his whole Bob Marley collection. As the night wore on, the guests mimicked his accent and the way he moved. The coach party, now sporting bright red faces, remained on the grass to cool their sunburn. As they swayed, they appeared like a clump of giant tulips affected by a breeze. Two members of the troupe, whose conversation was now almost incoherent, pondered their predicament. Eyes wandering wildly, and having little or no control over their mouths, they communicated very slowly.

"We gonna sit 'ere all neet?"

"If tha wants."

"I'll have to go, but a can't get up"

"Get driver to tek us 'ome?"

"I am the feckin' driver."

"Oh, well, if we can't get 'ome, it must be time for another."

They attempted to help each other up, but their legs were in a worse state than their mouths.

"Uze round is it?"

"Whoever can stand, I'd say."

They grinned, then whispered, and then grinned again.

"Ants, ants, big red ants!" they shouted.

A comrade, who was only perhaps one per cent less drunk, scrambled to his feet.

"Your round, your round!" they shouted and pointed.

Inside the club, the low lighting and atmospheric beat of the Rasta music was having a hypnotic effect on those on the crowded dance floor. Benjamin was fascinated by the control he had. He was able to control their movements and their voices. As the tempo and temperature rose, he felt able to control their minds. He was under the impression that the majority, mainly women, would have followed him to the ends of the earth, or at least to the nearest patch of long grass.

At the bar, the conversation revolved around the quality of the beer, the convivial social atmosphere, and the fact that within months it would all be gone. The anger created by the injustice of the situation was reaching lynch mob proportions.

"What gives him the right to take this off us?" remonstrated Arthur.

He waved his arms about to indicate the size of the building. But, as he was still holding a pint of beer, all he managed was to soak them through. The circle of friends nodded approval and backed away.

As Susan retreated she backed, as though pre-arranged, into Tom Deakin.

"Can I have a word?" he said mysteriously.

"What's your problem?" she replied uneasily. They stepped away from the circle.

"Well actually, it's not my problem," he coughed.

She looked at him blankly. "Come on, say your piece."

He rummaged in his pocket, and then produced what in the dimness of the disco lights looked like a small discarded piece of cloth.

"I believe these are yours. You left them in the shed."

The obscure lighting not only concealed the sight of a petite article of underwear, but also the reddening of her face.

"How do you know they're mine, could be anybody's," she said, almost stunned into silence.

"Give me some credit," Tom replied bluntly, and walked away.

She deftly stuffed the skimpy item, especially bought for the occasion, back in her bag.

"Think positive," she muttered. "Thought I'd lost them."

Around midnight, Roland cruised past in his car and was shocked to see the revelry continuing. He reached for his mobile phone. Modern technology has created the ability to make immediate contact with others all around the world, but this is based on a simple premise that they are willing and able to accept your call. Roland was only a hundred yards away from the person he wished to speak to, but the simple premise had failed. He could have actually walked up to where the phone was ringing. But the melodic bleep emitting from the phone was rendered ineffective, beneath the comatose body of the leader of rent-a-mob. He was where he had been most of the day, lying on the grass. Roland waited a while, and then spun the rear wheels, as his patience gave out. He headed to his office and decided to get some inspiration from a bottle of ten-year-old malt. The more he drank, the greater was his desire to "sort this matter out" and alongside, heightened his courage to do so. He returned to the cricket club much later after most of the revellers had gone home, but this time on foot and carrying a can of petrol.

The pavilion was a wooden structure supported by a three-layer row of bricks, with one in every ten removed to provide a through-flow of air. He made a funnel from some old cardboard and poured the petrol through the gaps in the bricks. The petrol soaked into the mass of litter and dried grass that had accumulated over the years. He systematically worked along one end, then across the back and finally along the other end. He decided against treating the front for fear of being spotted.

"Too risky. Always be some bastard who can't sleep," he said under his breath.

When he had finished, he put the lid on the can. To his horror, he discovered that in his efforts to do the job quickly, he had also doused his shoes, socks and trousers in petrol. A vision of himself in a ball of flame flashed through his mind, he even saw the ironic headline: *ARSONIST BURNED ALIVE. CLUBHOUSE SAVED.*

"No option," he thought as he removed his trousers.

He rummaged in his pockets for the matches, placed his trousers neatly folded under a hedge, then crept back barefoot to the walkway between the shed and the clubhouse. He was building up the nerve to strike the match, when he heard voices from inside the shed. He dropped the unlit match and held his breath. After a moment, curiosity got the better of him. He gingerly moved over to the shed and put his ear to the door. The noises from within puzzled him.

"Wha, wha, ooh, ooh, Jesus Christ."

'Religious meeting, this hour, in a garage?' he mused.

"Oh, good God!" the voice continued.

Even more intrigued, he edged closer. He wasn't to know that the rusty metal door was not quite shut. As he pressed his ear against it, the door clanged against its metal frame. Fearing discovery and using his old maxim, 'leg it while you can', he set off across the pitch. But legging it across the pitch wasn't one of his best ideas. Even though it took Benjamin a few seconds to disentangle himself from his latest conquest, he still had time to spot the half-naked figure before it disappeared down the road.

"Bare-arsed streaking across the pitch? Usually they do it during the game," he said, desperately trying to reassure the lady who now had totally gone off the idea of a shed full of tools doubling as a bedroom.

The commotion roused one of the rent-a-mob crew, who was shivering with cold, having crashed out for the night on the grass.

"A piss, another beer and a warmer place to doss. Simple necessities," he muttered as he headed towards the pavilion.

The lock on the door was a simple matter for someone who could break into a Land Rover 4x4 in ten seconds. Then, having satisfied his first priority, he stumbled in the darkness towards the bar ~ only to find it shuttered up.

"More subtlety required for this," he said smashing a chair through the one of the flimsy hardboard sections.

He flicked on the light switch behind the bar. As the fluorescent flickered on, his eyes were dazzled by the display of so many different ways of poisoning his liver. He pulled the lever on the beer pump, but nothing happened. Disappointment, then elation, swept over his face as he spotted a door marked cellar. He pushed it opened put his hand round the corner and felt for the light switch and flicked it on. It was the last movement to be made under his own effort. The petrol fumes had filled the cellar. It was only a small spark from the old light switch, but just enough to ignite the explosion that both spiritually and physically transported him heavenwards. A split second before he expired, he could not believe his rotten luck.

A few hours later, the cold light of day displayed the full effect of the blast. A pile of smouldering rubble was all that remained. Onlookers watched the firemen prod the hot bricks and charred wood. Meanwhile, a lone policeman, notebook at the ready, scribbled statements.

"Thout it were gonna take off, all this flame from underneath. It actually lifted off the ground," said a female witness, who wished to remain anonymous.

"Gas leak," said a fireman.

"Aye, got to be gas," confirmed another.

"No soddin gas on," said John Appleby first to arrive.

"Oh… right," said the fire chief.

"Rotten stink. Is it beer or petrol?"

"Mmm… not quite sure. They both smell alike and have the same effect," said John, trying to make light of the situation.

A fireman in the middle of the rubble poked something soft. As he prodded harder, the end of his stick took on a crimson colour.

"Sarg, sarg!" he shouted. "Think we 'ave a casualty."

The policeman looked up, flipped over another page in his book and moved closer.

Within minutes, the area was cordoned off. Blue lights flashed, and where previously there had been no particular interest, now it seemed as though every blade of grass would be looked under.

As John stared in disbelief, Craig Jakeson approached on a brand new bike. He bravely cycled clean across the pitch.

"Bit of a mess," he said, grinning from ear to ear.

John turned round and immediately put two and twenty-two together.

Across the way, the Bradley and Perkins families surveyed their blast-affected bungalows. Albert raised his hands in despair.

"Can you soddin' believe it? Put mesh up to save the windows from a ball and an explosion puts the whole bloody lot in. I don't think were insured for terrorist attack."

"Terrorist attack?" queried his wife.

"Place was full of anarchists yesterday. Two coach-loads. It'll be them as planted the bomb."

Geoffrey deliberated: "But why the cricket club?"

Just then, Susan ran over from the pitch: "They've found a body in the rubble, one of them lads off the coach."

"What did I say? It probably went off as he was planting it," said Albert.

His wife turned to him, highly embarrassed. "Shut up you fool," and promptly dragged him inside.

Alison clutched at Geoffrey's leg. "Don't like it here any more Daddy."

He looked down at her picked her up and carried her away from the remains of the front door:

"Me neither love. That's why we're having a few days away while they fix this lot."

The 'Treatment' Continues

The aromatherapy cure for Sir Alf's incapacity was working, but only slowly.

"Have to increase the reps, the intensity, and maybe change the oil" advised Flora.

"Suits me, what are reps?" he said as he swung himself on the bed.

As the massaging of the aromatic oils and relaxing music got underway, Sir Alf and Flora drifted into their own mindless thoughts, unaware of a taxi making its way up the drive.

Miriam paused just before opening the door. She peered up at the sky. It had clouded over. Although it didn't look like rain, it looked cold and damp. She wondered why the hell she had come back.

Literally hours ago, she was bathed in the clear blue sky and sunshine of Majorca. In fact, it was this very taxi that had taken her to Manchester Airport just four short weeks ago. Totally hacked off with the goings on at home, she immediately responded to a bronzed middle-aged lady's advice at her health club: "The sun, sea, red wine and the Spaniards… it'll take years off you. Just bugger off before you think too hard about it."

So she did bugger off. She left a note giving little detail of her intentions, just saying, 'I'm going away'. She also followed the other bit of advice that was offered: "Teck nowt but your credit card." It was an early morning flight when she left. 'Even better,' she thought as she quietly closed the door. 'Less explaining to do.'

She felt odd going away and not having to carry a case. "Just passport, tickets and Visa," she muttered as she checked her handbag for the third time. She had asked the taxi driver to pick her up at the end of the drive. As she walked with her back to the house, she felt like she was leaving for good. It was a good feeling, exciting, if a little weird.

The flight was shorter than she anticipated. Just time for a coffee, a glance at the duty free, and then the announcement came that they were about to land. She noticed during the flight that while the cloud cover was very thick over the UK, it was clear as a bell across the Channel.

"No wonder we're all depressed and they're all happy," she said to the woman sitting next to her. Her fellow passenger offered only a simpering smile of acknowledgement over the top of a thick novel.

As she stepped out of the plane and made her way down the steps, she couldn't help but notice that everyone was smiling. 'Amazing what a bit of sun does to 'em,' she thought. She felt uplifted as she made her way through the *Nothing to Declare* gate and couldn't resist a comment.

"Could tell you a thing or two," she said to the uniformed guard who totally ignored her.

But what really made her day was when she saw her name on a placard being held aloft by a very smooth and tanned young man. She felt elated. She let him prattle on as they drove to the hotel, whilst she stared through the window.

The scenery of steep valleys and quaint villages fascinated her as it all too swiftly whizzed by. The driver casually screeched round the narrow roads that all seemed to have perilous drops into the sea. Although she had fastened the safety belt, she clung onto the straps.

"Slow down for God's sake ~ unless you want my breakfast all over your seats!" she barked at the driver. He spoke little English but got the message from the terror and volume of her voice.

She had got the accommodation out of the 'Bijou and Friendly' brochure, but was a little apprehensive. As she pointed out to the travel agent: "Do I read tiny and over-bearing for bijou and friendly."

The driver turned off the main road and freewheeled downhill, then straight into the cobbled courtyard of an old, but well-kept, hotel. As she stepped out of the taxi however, she was overwhelmed with praise.

"It's bloody gorgeous," she said, as she paid the taxi driver.

She wandered to the end of the courtyard, through a stone archway and looked out over the rocky shoreline. She shaded her eyes from the bright sun with her hand, and could see small yachts circling the island.

"I wonder what they're thinking," she pondered, as she watched them slowly disappear out of sight.

Following a path sheltered by orange and lemon trees, she wandered towards a private pool with a small bar. As she approached, a waiter anticipated her thoughts.

"Fresh orange juice with ice?" he inquired.

"Grand," she concurred.

The waiter, who had not come across this expression before, tilted his head.

Luckily, a voice from behind, interpreted: "Si, por favor." The interpreter held out his hand in welcome. "Mrs Bullock?" he said in a Middle English accent.

Miriam hesitated at the formality, then gushed, "What a place you've got here."

They chatted and exchanged pleasantries, then the host suggested:

"Can I help you with your luggage? You must be tired after your journey."

She looked at the table slightly embarrassed. She had taken her friend's advice, but on the flight had pondered this very predicament.

"It's like this…"

At the very moment that she hesitated, he put his index finger to his lips.

"You don't have to explain anything to me. You're here to relax and enjoy yourself. It's my duty to see that everything's in place, in order for that to happen."

Then he smiled in a way that Miriam thought was very sincere.

He showed her to her room and opened the balcony double doors.

"I thought you might appreciate a sea view," he said.

She looked round at the sumptuous furnishings. It was everything she tried to create at home.

"I must go out to buy some essentials," she said as she opened the walk-in wardrobe.

"Ah," he said, looking at his watch. "They'll all be closed now."

Then he smiled again, "That kind of shopping usually takes place in the evening when the sun cools and the lights go on. It's a much better atmosphere. Can I get one of the ladies in our employ to show you the best shops?"

Miriam hesitated, "I'd much prefer if you could accompany me. Would you mind? You seem to have such good taste."

"It'd be my pleasure. In the meantime, relax. There are towelling robes for your use in the drawers. If you fancy a snack, the waiter will organise it for you."

After he had gone, she lay back on the king-sized bed and stared up at the chandelier. "Am I dreaming or what?" she whispered.

It took a few days for her to acclimatise and find her way around. She tested the bus and taxi service and decided that the public transport was fine.

'I'm not in any rush, so what's it matter how long it takes?' she thought as she tried to fathom the bus timetable. She bought a large straw hat from the market. It was larger than most, and a trifle colourful, but she felt fine. "Couldn't get away with this at home," she told the lady as she handed over the money. The lady smiled, not having understood a single word.

She was strolling by the shore, wearing the big hat and a flowing sarong that she obtained from the same market, when she realised that she wasn't angry any more. She felt physically relaxed, for the first time in years.

Each day she would get the bus further and further afield. "So much to see," she said to Arthur, the host, when they planned her next excursion. She had a thing about markets and would coincide the trip to match the day of the market in each town.

"Do be careful. There are people who frequent markets who prey on, how shall I say, obviously affluent individuals such as yourself. They pick your pockets, sell you fakes, and misuse your Visa card. Never let it out of your sight," Arthur warned.

She felt the warmth of his concern: "Thanks for looking out for me, I do appreciate it." As she spoke, she inadvertently placed her hand on his knee. Neither of them seemed concerned.

As her ventures got further and further away, so her return to the hotel became later and later. One day she arrived back after the evening meal. "Tell me to mind my own business if you like but..." Arthur paused as he offered her a glass of red wine. "I worry... a lady on her own... not familiar with the area... would you mind if I give you this?" he pushed a small mobile phone towards her.

"Oh Arthur, you do look after me."

"It lights up," he enthused. "So you can see what you're doing."

In the fading light, the phone shone in her hand. She grinned as she looked at the display.

"You'll have to show me how to use it."

"I'll take that as a yes," he said. "You must be hungry?"

"I thought dinner had finished?"

"It's ok. I'll prepare for us a typical Spanish dinner."

"Can I help? I used to work in a kitchen... twenty five years ago."

They went into the kitchen.

"Size of them pans," she enthused.

"Paella pans," he answered.

He reached for a smaller double-handed pan that was clean on the inside, but looked like it had been rescued from a house fire on the outside.

"Paella for two?"

"Right then," she grinned, donning an apron.

They took the plates of rice chicken and seafood and sat on the plastic chairs that surrounded the pool. He beckoned the waiter and spoke to him in Spanish. Minutes later, the waiter returned with an ice bucket containing, as he described it: "a local vintage modelled after my physique, smooth and well rounded." Miriam laughed heartily as his dry humour continued throughout the meal.

"Do you know I haven't laughed like this in years," she said.

As the humour subsided, he ordered another bottle.

"Your Spanish is so good," she enthused.

"You have to practice. If you can't speak the lingo, you either starve or pay a fortune for everything."

"How long have you been practising?"

"Fifteen years."

"You've been here fifteen years?" she said with disbelief.

"I've been in worse places," he responded.

"On your own?"

"Came out with my wife. We bought this place as a wreck ~ took ages to do it up. That was the undoing of us. She went back home after two years, left me to it. When it was finished, she wanted a divorce and half of what the hotel was worth. Well, by that time it was worth few bob, but I'd no option but to get a loan or sell up. Glad I didn't... Tell me about you," he said as he topped up their glasses.

Miriam took a deep breath.

"Good God where do I start?" she pondered.

"Here," he said holding out his glass. To you and your holiday."

They touched glasses and she toasted, "To you and your idyllic hotel."

He listened intently, and they kept eye contact, as she explained how the past twenty odd years had been a 'disappointment, to say the least'. He refilled her glass at an opportune moment.

"Am I going on too much?"

He did not speak, just smiled and shook his head.

"So you see," she said as she finished, "What I've had to put up with."

"How on earth could he ignore your needs, your charm?" he said smoothly.

"Do you know I've had these thoughts running round in my head for years. Not once have I found anyone I could tell. I've only known you for a few days."

"The Spanish air," he laughed, "It works wonders for your tongue."

"Not only your tongue." She pushed forward the key to her room. "This duty of yours, how far does it go?"

Back to Reality

"Don't go away…" she ordered the taxi driver.

Leaving her bags on the porch, she entered the house and immediately sniffed the aromatic atmosphere,

"Jesus…what the hell am I doing here?" she cussed.

She cocked an ear to the music emitting from the relaxation tape.

Such was the distraction of the therapy, they failed to notice Miriam standing in the bedroom doorway. She coughed loudly to gain their attention.

Flora looked up at Miriam and yelped, then stared straight at her. She couldn't think of anything appropriate to say, so said nothing.

Sir Alf looked up at her and smiled, as though to say, "Don't worry," Sir Alf raised himself up on his elbows.

"Been there long have you? Seen enough?" he snapped.

"Plenty, but I thought I'd seen everything," she sniggered.

"It's not what you think," said Flora getting upset.

"No?" Miriam questioned.

"It's part of his treatment," Flora added.

"For what?" Miriam shouted with disbelieving laugh in her voice.

"To me, it looks like you taking advantage of a man with no legs but plenty of cash."

"You bitch!" he growled. He hoisted himself up and swung round till his legs hung over the edge. "She's done more for me in a couple of months than you did all the years we were married." He slid off the bed and stood on the floor.

"See this? I'd still be in the bloody chair if it were left to you!" he ranted.

"Dead right you would! See you in court, you and your lady ~ cos you'll be the main witness," she hissed at Flora.

"Don't mind yourself over her," Sir Alf reassured Flora after his wife had stormed out. "This bust up has been on the cards for a while. Just sorry you had to be here when it happened."

Flora smiled thinly.

They stood there for a minute, not speaking, just mulling over their own predicament. The phone ringing in the hall cut short any verdict.

"I'll get it," said Flora and dashed off.

Sir Alf pulled on his trousers, and then grinned.

"Day started ok, got even better, and then went down the pan. What the hell!"

"Terry Cargill for you."

"Man must be bloody psychic," he quipped. With the aid of two crutches, he hobbled into the other bedroom and took the call.

"Just about to call you, you must be a mind reader."

Terry sounded sombre. "You've heard then."

"Heard what?"

"About your Roland. He's being questioned by the police."

"Him and his bleeding fast cars, I knew him they'd get him in trouble."

"Got nothing to do with fast cars. It's about the club burning down, sodding serious this. They found a body. He's in deep shit if you ask me."

"Did I say the day was going down the pan?" he muttered. "I'll meet you at the station, soon as I'm ready. Oh, by the way… I need you to sort out a divorce…"

"All change, eh?" Terry commiserated.

"You don't know half of it," he replied putting down the phone before he had finished.

John's 'Bad Luck' Continues

"Thanks for coming, don't know anyone else to talk to," John Appleby confided in Tom Deakin.

"No problem. Glad to help."

They were sitting in the kitchen. As John poured the tea, he was physically shaking. "I'm sure it was meant for me."

"What was?"

"This prank ~ another. It killed the old chap next door this morning. I'm sure it were meant for me."

Tom sat listening in disbelief.

"Early hours, this awful racket on the door just like last time. Thought I'd get the bastard this time. Tried to open it, but it'd only open a bit. Mine and next door's knockers were tied together.

It must have disturbed the old chap next door. He must have tried to open his door. Course it wouldn't. When I tried to open my door, it shut his door, and so on... went on for ages. I could hear him shouting. He must have panicked. No other way out of these back-to-backs. Then it all went quiet. They found him dead behind the door."

"Frigging hell," was all Tom could say.

Banner Problem

Down at The Throttle Flyer Arnold Bosworth was sitting at his desk mulling over a pleasant predicament.

"What do you reckon, Martin?" he asked his sub-editor, who was really just a dogsbody with a posh title. "Should we go with the cricket club fire or the death of the pensioner at the hands of a prankster?"

The sales of the paper had risen dramatically recently. Arnold, of course, put this down to his hard-hitting, no-nonsense front page banner headline. So, as usual, he decided to go with the most sensational one-liner he could devise.

"*Body found in gutted club... gutted body found in club... c*lubbed body found in gutt*ed... prank death shocks town....* Nah, too soppy... Got it!" he yelled.

But Martin was no longer listening.

"*Who's Next?...* Big letters, big question mark. That should put the shits up them. Nice to have something to get me teeth into."

That afternoon, as the printing press ran at blinding speed to get the paper on the stands, Martin eavesdropped on a conversation Arnold didn't appear to want.

"You stupid little shit, I told you not to ring here... A better bike, you must be joking! Look, can't talk here, I'll give you a ring ok... Don't ever call here again."

With that, he slammed down the phone, looked round, and his mind went into overdrive.

Same Police Station, Different Interviewee

"Mr Bullock, can you account for your petrol-stained trousers being found near the scene of the burnt out cricket club?" inquired the detective.

"No," Roland responded.

"Did you pour petrol around the club with the intention of..." his question was cut short by the sniggering of the young constable supposed to be standing to attention.

"Something wrong constable?" the detective barked.

"No sir," he replied.

But the giggles had got the better of him.

"Explain yourself outside."

The detective followed the constable, who was now just short of having a convulsion, out of the room. Roland sat in silence, and then looked at the door as laughter erupted from the other side.

Ten minutes later, the detective re-entered the room. The red eyes bore witness to the fact that he had eventually got the two-week-old joke and the significance of the motif.

"Shall we continue... *Mr err Bullock.*"

That afternoon Sir Alf met Terry Cargill in his office.

"Where do we start?" he asked.

Sir Alf looked stunned.

"Everything's falling apart," he muttered wringing his hands and staring at the floor.

"Let's take it one stage at a time. This way, we're less likely to miss anything," he said reassuringly. "First, Roland. They seem to have a strong case, but it's based on circumstantial evidence. No one actually saw him light a match, even though it looks certain that he did pour the petrol under the club house."

"He'll go down then," sighed Sir Alf.

"Early days yet. They'll have to prove that he set fire to the club to prove manslaughter. Could be arson or just damage to property. Going to be tricky though."

"Jesus... manslaughter... arson! Never thought I'd hear those words relating to me and mine." He cupped his hands round his head.

"About the divorce," said Terry slightly louder than he intended.

"Been on the cards for years. But being caught out with the hired help kind of put the tin hat on it," said Sir Alf resignedly.

Terry grinned: "Not much wrong with you then." He sat back and straightened his professional face. "Knowing the lady as I do and the

151

probable mood she's in, she'll be after half. So what's it to be, the house or the works?"

Sir Alf, shocked, looked up. "Do I have a choice?"

"Look, I don't know all your financial details… but making an educated guess, I'd say your house must be worth a mint, and your lock-up units about the same, maybe more. She'll want half, so which do you want to sell to raise the cash?"

"Simple as that. Lifetime's work," he sighed.

Terry softened his voice and smiled. "Look… I know it's a bastard, but that's the way it is."

"Give me a day or two, will you? Serious thinking to do. Can you get me a cab?"

"It could be an awful lot worse," Terry said with a broadening grin. "There are folk out there who'd love to be in your shoes, especially when it comes to the hired help."

Sir Alf forced a smile, but didn't speak.

"Good to see you're on your feet again. It solves one problem," he added, pointing at Sir Alf's legs.

"Early days yet. They ache like bastards after a while. Not sure I can cope with going back to work yet," he said, pursing his lips and gripping his thigh.

"Leave Roland to me. I'll get on to you as soon as I hear anything," Terry added as Sir Alf hobbled to the door.

Sir Alf clambered into the back of a cab and they set off towards home. As they passed the cricket club, he saw the cordoned off remains of the building. Two days after the fire, onlookers were still staring at the blackened rubble hoping to spot something gruesome sticking out from the charred timbers.

"Funny do that," said the driver.

"Don't see anyone laughing," he snapped.

"I didn't mean it like that. What I was trying to say was, all that fuss over trying to keep the club going. No bugger goes anyway, and now it ends like this. It's like it were meant to be, if you get my drift."

Sir Alf would have replied, but he was mentally calculating the acreage. He let himself in and flopped into his wheelchair which was conveniently parked inside the door, then whizzed into the kitchen. He braked hard at the sight of the figure slumped head in arms at the breakfast table.

"Flora, didn't expect to find you here!"

"Felt awful about this morning, really awful," she said, her voice breaking up.

He moved forward and ruffled her hair.

"Hey don't you go worrying about this lot. There's lots of folk that wish they were in our position." He clicked on the kettle then after a pause added, "Apparently."

Flora, puzzled, looked up and grinned through mascara-stained eyes.

"Oh Alf, what are we going to do?"

He stared back, "Well actually, I thought we could finish off the oil from this morning."

That evening Sir Alf was resting. He felt warm and relaxed. Despite all the goings on, he felt ok with the world. He could even feel his legs. 'What a grand lass,' he thought as he reflected on the afternoon's treatment. He smiled as he remembered how they laughed at his remark about making good use of that oil. "Don't be rude," she had giggled as she wiped him down with a towel.

He was just drifting to sleep on the settee when he heard a knock at the front door.

"Bleeding hell's this?" he muttered as he grabbed his crutches, and then hobbled to answer it. "Good God!" he shouted as he stared at the doorframe. It looked like the Grim Reaper.

"Give somebody a soddin heart attack, doing a thing like that."

"Sorry Mr… Sir."

"Alf, just call me Alf."

"I didn't mean to scare you," reassured Benjamin.

"Come and talk in the kitchen."

Benjamin sniffed the air.

"There's a wicked fragrance in here."

"It's the polish. Cleaner's been today. Now what can I do you for?"

"Your Roland, he's been a bad ass to the club."

Sir Alf nodded, "Aye, aye."

"Point is, I can get him off the hook. But I'm not sure he deserves it."

Sir Alf looked at him sideways, in a manner that suggested, 'I know he's been a bad ass, but this is my son we are talking about.'

"Really?" he said.

"You see, I saw him leg it across the pitch at least an hour before the club went up."

"Oh!" Sir Alf responded. "How did you know it were him?"

"Aint many dudes round here can afford Kalvin Kline boxers. Oh, he left this behind too," he grinned as he held out a leather credit card holder with RB embossed in gold on the corner.

"Don't you think you should go to the police? They can have you for withholding evidence?"

"Oh, I'll be going. It's just when is the question. You see those down at the club have been very good to me, and I feel I should return the favour. So I've come here to talk man-to-man about the club's future."

"Now look, if you think you can blackmail me..." said Sir Alf, losing his temper.

"No, no, nothing like that, more... reassurance that's all. Keep cool," responded Benjamin holding up his hands.

"The only reassurance I can give you at this time is that there will be a decision, and it'll be made, let's say, with the village's best interest at heart."

"Seems fair enough. Can't ask for more than that."

He gave Sir Alf a panoramic view of his gleaming white teeth.

After Benjamin had gone, Sir Alf sat and pondered: "Well at least it won't be manslaughter... but it was close."

His emotions were mixed. He was glad his only son would be off the major charge.

"But he did pour the petrol under the club, and more luck than good judgement that he wasn't the one to set it off," he ranted to the empty house.

About the same time, in the back room of The Ram Inn:

"Sad do, sad do, what an awful waste," said Simon Jakeson to one of his mates.

"Did anyone know his name?" asked the friend.

"No, no, I'm on about all that ale going to waste. Don't think it could have survived all that heat, do you?"

Decision Time

Susan had recently sensed a change: her mood, her appetite but more important her monthly cycle. A tester bought from the local chemist indicated the reason and gave her a problem she could have done without.

"There was always an element of risk," she said to the mirror as she flushed the remains of the kit down the toilet. "But I'm afraid continuing is out of the question."

Later that day, she presented herself at Joe Lagg's front door.

"I'm still sick!" he shouted through the letterbox.

"You'll be more than sick, if you don't let me in," she replied.

"I'm still sick I tell you, bog off!"

"Do you know what they do to men like you in prison? First, they rape the shit out of them, then they…"

Susan heard the various chains and latches being undone.

"What's up for God's sake?" he said angrily as he closed the door behind them.

A couple of minutes later, he said: "Fifteen hundred quid, what the hell for?"

"Look, I'm not going to beat about the bush. I wouldn't ask if it weren't urgent."

"Just tell me why I should, that's all. All you've ever done is threaten me."

"Now look, if you want to join your mate, it can be arranged," Susan said wagging a finger at him.

"See… you're threatening me again."

She turned, grabbed the door handle and turned it in a feigned attempt to leave. To her relief, it worked.

"Ok, ok… though I don't know why."

She let go of the handle and smiled. "It's favour, doing a good turn. You'll feel much, much better afterwards…"

He was recovering from writing out the cheque, by sipping a strong cup of tea laced with whisky, when the doorknocker rattled again.

"Mrs Bullock… Come in why don't you."

But Miriam was already down the hall, by the time he had said "in".

"What the bloody hell are you two up to?"

"Which two?"

"Don't mess me about. I guessed before I went away that you two were putting pressure on the cricket club… so…"

"Nowt to do with me. I've been in my sick bed for two weeks. Ask Susan,"

"Susan? Susan who?"

"Oh… no-one."

"You're hiding something."

"I'm not… it's nowt to do with me, I keep telling you."

She gripped the top of his towelling robe, along with a good hand-full of chest hairs:

"You lard arse, you were always soft when you were a kid. Tell me the truth or I'll… I'll…"

Having just been harangued and fleeced out of fifteen hundred quid, in addition to feeling a trifle sickly and hard done by, his threshold of pain was at an all-time low. He had no option.

"Ok… ok… it were just a bit of fun."

Tea Break at The Throttle Flyer

Arnold was having a 'no news' day ~ at least not the type of news he wanted.

"More than you can cope with these days, eh," Martin said. Arnold was chewing his pen top along with a cold sausage sarnie.

"Oh," he muttered, licking some half-chewed bread off the cap of his biro.

Arnold pointed the damp end of his pen at Martin and lectured:

"Everyone knows about the sodding fire. No one's interested in some old git snuffing it behind a door. It's ordinary news, everyday ordinary news. It won't sell papers! But smut sells! Dirty goings on sells paper, what we need is some filth!" He said spitting sausage across his desk.

"Well, Lord and Lady Muck are splitting up and their lad's in the nick on suspicion of the club fire. It's all over the place."

"So?" Arnold replied unimpressed.

This was before Arnold's time, so the newly promoted sub-editor had to fill in the blanks.

"Apparently he's been having it away... they don't know who with...."

"Hang on... hang on, the guy's in a wheelchair... isn't he?"

Martin grinned and nodded.

Arnold sat up and with renewed vigour started scribbling headlines.

"Triangle, wheel, degrees, Mill man spins web of deceit. There's a line here somewhere, need more info."

An hour later he stood at the entrance to Sir Alf's house, pen and pad at the ready. Flora opened the door just a fraction and peeped out.

"Throttle Flyer here. Would Sir Alfred like to comment on the apparent collapse of his dynasty?"

As he spoke, he put his foot in the doorway, a trick that a Fleet Street journalist taught him. "While you're talking they don't watch your feet," he had been advised. But the other advice he forgot to take heed of was, "wear stout shoes, not trainers."

The well-worn trainers were no match for solid oak doors, especially when slammed by Flora whose arms had been strengthened by hours of massage.

"What's all the commotion?" said Sir Alf arriving to find the wily reporter holding his crushed foot.

"Says he's got dysentery, wants a comment."

"What do you want?" Sir Alf shouted down at him as he held his swelling foot.

"An ambulance."

"Don't know about an ambulance. Hard-boiled eggs used to do the trick. Get six of them in you and you'll not shit for weeks."

Flora looked at the reporter, then Sir Alf.

"Must be severe. Look at his face."

Sir Alf turned and grinned at Flora: "Well he's got his comment. Can you call him an ambulance, love?"

As the increasing pain racked up his leg, one flicker of a thought zapped through Arnold's brain. The word 'love' and the affectionate smile. "Gotcha..." He too grinned for a split second, and then the pain took over again.

Later, sporting a gleaming white plaster on his ankle, he sipped tea in the Milky Coffee Café. Meanwhile, his companion made slurping noises through a plastic straw as he reached the bottom of his milkshake.

"Can I write on it?" he asked, as he let the straw drop into the glass.

Still in some pain, Arnold was beginning to lose his patience.

"No you bloody well can't, now concentrate will you!"

"Want a new, better bike. This one's shite," Craig sulked.

"You'll get a new bike when you've done the work. Names and times, names and times," he repeated. "I want to know who goes where up at the Bullock house, got it?"

"Can I have another milkshake?"

Arnold closed his eyes and held the outside of the plaster cast.

No Hiding Place

"Alf… you seen that lad sitting in the bushes?"

"Aye… Been there a day or two now, just sits there. Could do with some lessons in espionage, if that's what he's up to."

They stared at him through the net curtains. He, in turn, stared back.

"I don't think he's there for the benefit of his health. I'll sneak out of the back, while you keep him occupied. Better take me stick."

Flora offered him his stick.

"Keep him occupied… How?" she asked.

"Use your initiative," he added with a dirty grin that she had not seen before.

"Oh… flattered I'm sure."

He got into his wheelchair and whizzed out of the back door.

Meanwhile, Flora placed a low table at the bedroom window and climbed on it. She drew back the net curtains and waved affectedly at the lad. She started to gyrate and could see his head nodding to her movements. She mouthed, exaggeratedly and slowly: "Want to see more?" She saw the binoculars go up and down, and then casually undid the buttons to her pinny. "More?" she inquired.

The binoculars shook, but in a general up and down fashion. She pulled at her blouse to reveal a portion of cleavage. It was then she saw the top of Sir Alf's head speeding down the lane towards the boy. "More?" she teased. She leaned forward and her sexy smile changed to a leer, as she pulled out her tongue and raised her middle finger.

The boy dropped his gaze to see Sir Alf racing towards him. He climbed on his bike and set off, but was swiftly overtaken by the powerful chair. As he drew alongside, Sir Alf shoved his walking stick through the front spokes. This had a dramatic effect on the progress of the bike and its rider. Both cart-wheeled into the grass verge.

Sir Alf edged the chair up against the stricken lad: "What you up to?" he shouted raising the stick up in the air.

Back at the house, he related the story to Flora.

"He were snooping for that bloody reporter. It's not funny you know," he added, noting Flora's smirk.

"I know it's not. I just enjoyed teasing him that's all. It's a good job you weren't any longer, I'd have been down to my smalls."

"If I'd have known that, I'd have hung on a bit."

"You've changed your tune. Must be the fresh air. Apparently it affects men of your age."

"Is it time for my aromatherapy yet?" Alf grinned as he grabbed her pinny.

A Couple of Days After the Fire

"The good news is the beer's ok," Tom advised as he gulped down the majority of his pint in one go.

"Like it were meant to be," added Janice glumly.

The committee had borrowed the back room of the pub for a meeting.

"Aye well… life goes on, I suppose."

"Unless you're one of them there anarchists."

"Aye, he didn't last long," Janice said.

Susan had been putting on a brave face since her away day, but her emotions and her knickers department were not one hundred percent.

Not getting a response, Janice repeated her comment: "No life at all, had he?"

"Sorry, mistake to come," Susan said through a flood of tears.

They watched her disappear through the door.

"You been upsetting her?" Tom asked.

Janice shook her head.

"Ben's off in a few days. We should show some appreciation."

The others grinned as John Appleby read their thoughts.

"A karaoke night."

"A tent."

"A marquee."

"A cleaner," added Janice.

"A meeting!" shouted Arthur Padstow.

Top Floor at The Throttle Flyer

"Bob! Hello, it's Alf Bullock."

There was a pause as Bob Riley, non-executive director of The Throttle Flyer, cast his mind back.

"Of course… How the hell are you? Bloody hell, it must be years…"

"Aye that's what everyone says. Beginning to think I've been on another planet."

"Good to hear from you, we must have a pint."

"Aye, grand idea, but it's not a social call."

There was another pause.

"Go on then."

"It's one of your men. He's been snooping up at the house. Or rather, his bleeding lap dog has. I'd appreciate it if he were stopped."

"Don't tell me ~ Arnold Boswell," Bob sighed.

"Well… aye," Sir Alf replied with a surprised jump in his voice.

"You're not the first. Silly bastard will have us in court next. I'll have his wings clipped, if not cut off all together."

"You're a gem, we must have that pint."

At the Café

"I only promised you a bike if you got the goods. So what have you got?"

Craig held his arm.

"The old git were going to hit me with his stick, had me pinned down with his chair. That were after he wrecked my bike. He put his stick through the wheel. It's knackered now."

"So what have you got?" Arnold repeated with no concern at all for the boy's health.

"Nothing."

"All that time… nothing!" growled Arnold. He gripped him by the shirt.

"And what did you tell him?"

"Nothing, honest."

"You lying little shit."

He pulled him closer by the lapels.

"If I find that you've…"

The discussion they were having had caused interest. So much so that other customers had tuned in, and the proprietor had stopped pouring tea, mid-order. Arnold looked round, let go of the lad's lapels, and smoothed out the creases.

"A new bike? Of course you can have one. What colour?"

Craig noticed the change in his fortune, but pushed his luck a little too far.

"You'd better, you twat ~ or I'll tell everyone what you've been up to."

Arnold rested his aching leg on the rail underneath the table. He contemplated his circumstances for a moment, then leaned forward and whispered, "Right, yes, new bike, I'll swap it for the old one tonight, but I can't be seen handing it over. Meet me at the viewpoint… about half nine."

Craig scraped back the chair and rushed out. As he fled through the door, Arnold scanned the menu.

"Should be dark by then," he muttered.

Having finished his mid-afternoon break, Arnold hobbled back to the office to be greeted by Martin who had a silly grin on his face.

"Don't sit down," he advised. "You're wanted, top floor."

Arnold grinned.

"Must be another bonus. I wasn't really expecting it till next month."

"Don't think so," said Martin.

An hour later, Arnold was sitting in his car in the car park.

"Sacked, me! The best bleeding reporter they ever had! The little bastard must have run right to them. Well it's him… then the sodding rest."

Among the Flowers and Singing Birds

Joe was beginning to feel much better. The antibiotics the doctor had prescribed had eventually worked. He still didn't know what the illness had been. When asked, he spoke of hallucinations, fever, and delirium. He was finding it difficult to remember the goings on of the past few weeks. In fact, he was enjoying his break so much that he contemplated never going back.

"Susan what's-her-name needs a job. She can sodding well have one ~ mine."

He leant back on the lounger and sipped his herbal tea. He closed his eyes and felt the warmth of the sun on his face. He listened to a skylark and began to drift. The glass in his hand started to tilt. Although subconsciously, he knew it was falling, he couldn't keep a grip of it. But then curiously, he felt it being supported.

"Don't drop your glass, Mr Lagg," said a gruff but familiar voice.

Panic-stricken, he opened his eyes to find the Jakeson brothers looking down on him, one on either side. Immediately, his heart pounded and beads of sweat burst from his forehead.

"Heck did you get in here?"

"We tried the front door, but no answer. Figured you'd be round here."

The sight of these rather large gentlemen, peering down at him made his breathing go haywire. Panting heavily, he stared upwards. The bright sunlight made him blink uncontrollably. He gripped the top of his dressing gown.

"Fuck do you want?" he screamed.

"About three grand was the figure mentioned, if our memory serves."

"What?" he screamed again.

The faces came closer. "You said three grand if the games are stopped and they don't get a Cup."

"Well they are... and they won't," said the other brother. The brothers looked at one another to consider the last statement. They thought long and hard, nodded agreement, and then carried on.

"When do we get our money?"

"You'll have to give me some time. The man with the cash is in jail."

"No. You get the money or we'll do some alterations cos that's what we do. We're good at alterations. We can start by making this place look like the fucking cricket club, then we'll alter you."

The other brother, eager to have a say, chipped in:

"Yeah, like, err, the hunch back of Notre Dame, cos he's ugly."

The other brother shook his head, then looked at Joe.

"Fancy being ugly, do you?"

Joe shook his head.

"Twenty four hours then."

As they passed through the gate, Joe started to shake. So much in fact, that he dropped his glass.

Still in Charge

Susan was slowly coming to terms with what had happened over the past few months. She was staring at the aquarium screensaver on the computer, with a cup of coffee gripped between both hands. As the fish went round and round, so did her thoughts: cricket club, house, Benjamin, Geoffrey, Alison. She was unaware of the damage that could be caused by dripping hot coffee onto a keyboard, but a customer she had chosen to ignore, advised her:

"It'll never work again."

The familiar, but unexpected, voice caused her to spill the remainder of her cup.

"Now it'll definitely never work again," said Benjamin grinning.

"Benjamin... how are you?"

"Fine... fine. How are you?" he returned the question. "You aint been around."

"Oh, you know... what with the fire and everything... hadn't had the heart."

"I thought I better come round cos there's something weird happening."

As he spoke, there was a confused expression on his face. Susan could have sworn she saw his eyes watering.

"Come in the back, I'll put the kettle on."

She locked the door and changed the sign to closed then led him into the back office. They pulled the chairs close and sipped coffee.

"Thing is," said Benjamin with a croak in his voice, "I've left stacks of clubs in the past, but I aint never had the feelings I've got now. I can't sleep, I'm all churned up." He held her hand and sniffed. "I aint never felt like this before. I've even gone off my food. That aint like me."

Susan smiled and sniffed back a tear, then stroked his face,

"Oh Ben," she sighed.

Meanwhile, at the front of the office, Geoffrey was hovering at the locked door. He tried cupping his hands and peering through the window. He looked at his watch, and then tried squinting through the glass again.

"It clearly says closed, when it should be open," said a voice from behind.

Geoffrey turned to see Joe Lagg.

"Oh... you."

"Luckily, I have a key," he replied, ignoring Geoffrey's sneer.

"Glad to see somebody's lucky."

"Yes, yes, ok," said Joe, inserting the key in the door.

"Where's Susan?" Geoffrey asked. "She should be here and this place should be open."

They both looked at the light coming from under the door of the back room. Susan and Benjamin had heard the door being opened and both voices. They looked at each another.

"They won't understand ~ hide!" she hissed.

When the door opened, she was sitting at Joe's desk holding some papers. "Oh hello, thought I heard the door."

"You ok?" asked Geoffrey.

"Oh yes, just thought I'd catch up on some paperwork. It's easier if I just close for ten minutes."

"We never close," said Joe curtly.

Geoffrey gripped his arm. "Good idea, you'll get less disturbance that way."

"I need a key from the drawer."

Hastily she pulled open the drawer and handed Joe a large bunch of keys.

"Here," she said raising her voice.

Joe went into the corner, paused then turned: "Look away," he instructed, and then fumbled with the lock of a large old oak bureau. It matched the desk in size, which was fortunate for Benjamin and his six feet six frame, as he was crouched in the kneehole.

As they spoke, he felt peculiarly safe and wrapped his arms around Susan's legs and rested his head on her knees. She leaned over the top of the desk and placed her elbows on the blotting pad so that the top of his head would not show. Geoffrey was not used to seeing Susan in this official capacity. He was impressed by the way she sat at the desk, leaning forward, glasses perched on the end of her nose, pen in hand, effectively wielding power. So impressed was he, that he remained silent, dumbstruck. His imagination was just getting into gear when...

"Geoffrey?" she said alerting his attention.

He looked round, blinked and tried to respond.

"Yes... oh yes. We've got to go to the school. Alison's been hurt, nothing much, just a graze. They said we might want to take her to the hospital, just to be safe."

"For God's sake! So why are we dawdling here?"

The noise of Benjamin's head hitting the top of the desk was lost in her abuse of Geoffrey for not telling her earlier about Alison. She ushered both Geoffrey and Joe towards the door.

"Come on!" she hurried, raising her voice. She looked at Joe who was hesitating. "Come on... It won't matter if it's shut till tomorrow."

Once at the threshold, she uttered a cryptic message to Benjamin who was now rubbing his head and having serious second thoughts about a relationship.

"I'll carry on with this when I come back tomorrow… about nine!" she shouted, apparently to an empty room.

Joe and Geoffrey exchanged puzzled looks, but put it down as the rantings of a disturbed woman. They went their separate ways at the door, Geoffrey running behind Susan, and Joe clutching a manila envelope.

Benjamin waited till the voices faded, then crawled out from under the desk.

"Now that was close," he said grinning and straightening his clothes.

Craig was sitting on the boulders, near the viewpoint. He was sweating after having had to push the twisted bike all the way up the hill. The real part he hated though was the constant ribbing from people he passed on the way up. They laughed and pointed and gave him all kinds of advice on the correct way of riding it. But now he was here with his bike, but the other person, was not. He repeatedly looked at his watch.

"He said half nine," he muttered.

In fact, Arnold was not far away, in a lay-by on the way up the hill. He too looked at his watch, "Shit! It's still light. I'll give it another ten minutes," he grumbled.

It was ten o'clock before he thought it dark enough to make a move. Craig, however, had decided to call it quits and was on his way down by then. Arnold raced up the hill and caught Craig in his headlights.

"Got you, you little shit!" he shouted as he veered his car across the road. "Grass me up with my boss would you!" he shouted.

Craig wasn't aware at first that he had become a target. He just stepped back a bit from the road. Then, as the car came straight for him, he let go of his bike and started to run back up the hill. He heard a crunch and scraping noise as the car went over the bike. He paused for a fraction of a second and thought he recognised the wild eyes of Arnold staring through the windscreen.

Arnold did not pause though. The accelerating car hoisted Craig over the bonnet and across the windscreen. Arnold wrenched at the steering wheel in an attempt to shake Craig off the car. With the lad obscuring his view, he drove off the road and down the steep embankment. He hung on to the wheel as the car ripped through deep bracken. Then, with a mighty bang, it halted as it hit a track to a farmhouse.

Arnold awoke hours later cold, sore and very damp. He gripped the steering wheel as if the car was still moving. Then, as realisation set in, he looked around. Ignition and lights still on. The windscreen was cracked. He was not sure if he did it, or Craig, but his head ached like crazy. He looked at his watch. Just after midnight. He tried the engine. It spluttered into life, but was strangely loud.

"Fucking exhaust," he cursed.

He pressed the clutch with his good foot, tried to put it in gear, and then yelped.

"Jesus have I done!"

He tried again, this time using both hands. He edged the car forward to straighten it up, then reversed back along the track. As it swung round, the headlights picked out a shape in the bracken. He knew what it was and ignored it. Gingerly, and as quietly as he could, he reversed all along the track and back onto the road. He drove up the hill and spotted the remains of the bike. It still had sections of gleaming new paint, but its basic shape was now that of a banana. He got out of the car and limped towards the bike. Everything hurt and his trousers stuck to him. He looked down in disgust. He dragged the bike, and as best he could, and sent it down the hill.

"Here's your bike, you little shit!"

He locked the car in the garage and hobbled into the house. As he put the bolt on the door, he sputtered: "That's one done then."

Does Anyone Know?

It was a good few days before Arnold dared venture out, but the lack of basic sustenance and the desire to scour The Throttle Flyer got the better of him.

The swelling had receded in his hand and, with the help of a bottle of pills, his headache had gone. So it was time to set foot, even if it was a soggy foot because he forgot to protect the plaster from the shower, into the big outside world. He hobbled round to the garage and opened the up and over door.

"Jesus!" he exclaimed as he saw the wreck that used to be his car. "If I go out in this I'm dead."

He slammed down the door, after retrieving the aluminium crutch the hospital had lent him, and set off to the shop. It was curious, he thought, that when you wanted to be incognito everyone noticed you, and when you were feeling in need for human contact, nobody did. The man in the newsagents who normally would not give Arnold the time of day suddenly wanted to talk.

"How'd you do that? he asked pointing to the plastered ankle. "And that?" pointing to the brightly coloured bruise on his forehead.

"Oh… just… just give me a Flyer."

"Buying one. What for? You writes 'em, don't you?"

Arnold looked away for a moment, the disdain for the man clearly showing.

"Look, are you going to sell me one or what?"

Immediately, the headache returned. He held his head with one hand and his crutch with the other. He thought the plastic clip on the crutch would stay secured to his arm, but no. As he rummaged for change, the crutch clattered to the floor. The vendor on the other side of the counter added to the predicament by holding out the rolled up paper.

"God's sake," Arnold hissed.

Unable to stand unaided, he rested on the counter panting and his temperature rising. He reached down for his crutch but it was too far away. An old lady behind picked up the crutch and held it out to him. He nodded, and then resented the thought of being aided by a pensioner.

"Get off, I can manage!" he snapped.

But he couldn't. He hadn't enough hands, so he just tipped out a pile of loose change, snatched the paper and shuffled out.

"Ungrateful git," said the lady.

Unable to resist, he leant against a wall and scoured the paper for any news of the other night. He flicked the pages impatiently, till he got to the back page. *Mystery Hit and Run* ran the headline.

"Boring banner," he muttered.

He skimmed the comment for any implication. He got right to the end then: A police spokesman said that although they have no idea about the car or identity of the driver, the *vehicle* would be considerably damaged and the driver *would have sustained injuries.*

He was mulling over the possible sequence of events, when he started to race back through the paper.

"Yes!" he shouted.

Farewell Party for Club Pro ~ All Welcome.

Tea Time at the Perkins' House

"Are we going to the 'do' on Saturday?" posed Geoffrey.

"Not keen," replied Susan.

"Oh come on, we're supplying the beer. A new one ~ Winter Wonderland it's called."

"But it's summer."

"Aye well, we have to try 'em out. It might as well be on this shower."

"That's not very nice. These people are your neighbours."

"Yeah, I know, but I still feel like a bleeding stranger."

"You get on well with Albert."

"Oh thanks. Mr Happy as he's better known."

Susan had moved over to the sink and her mind started to drift. Her mind and her internals had started to get back to where they were a few months before. In her thoughts, she was reluctant to rehash it all again. 'But it was exciting. Plots, intrigue, subterfuge plus a bit on the side,' she mulled.

"Well are we going or what?"

"I don't know. You take Albert. It'll be good for him."

Geoffrey went over and put his arm round Susan's waist.

"You did look well the other day, sitting behind that desk all officious. Never seen you look like that. It's a good job what's his face was there or I'd have been round that desk like a shot."

For a split second, Susan raced through the possibilities.

"Good job you didn't," she croaked.

As their last duty, the committee had met to discuss the 'leaving do' for Benjamin. They sat around two tables pulled together in the pub. John Appleby's posture stiffened.

"As this is the last formal meeting we can dispense with the official procedure, I presume."

The others breathed a sigh of relief. But as he stood up and held out a paper, they knew he was going to have the last word.

"If I can just… I've written a little farewell speech."

"God's sake, save it for the leaving do!" the rest of the committee urged in unison.

"What a do! Free beer, booze till it runs out, and no cleaning up afterwards," he said mockingly, pointing at Janice. "Fancy tent as well."

"Do you mind? A marquee!" Janice pulled him up.

"Whatever. Let's go out with a bang,"

The others winced at his unfortunate comment, but did not rise to the bait.

The whole village turned up for the leaving do.

"What about me speech?" John said, his voice lost in the beat of music.
"Better get out there before it's too late."

He climbed up on the makeshift stage, and without asking Benjamin who was busy 'mixing', he grabbed the microphone.

"Kin 'ell, he never learns," said Tom, shouting to the others.

John tapped the microphone in time-honoured tradition, and then blew on it.

"Can we 'ave some hush for a minute."

It took ages for the revellers to quieten down.

"Just want to say... we did our best, but as you can see events conspired against us..." He paused momentarily as the events of the last few months flashed by. But patience was not a quality used to describe Throttle residents and mutterings began. On hearing this, he continued: "Aye, it's thanks to Benjamin here and the lads for giving it their best shot. Glad to see so many people have turned up. Maybe we should just organise leaving dos."

The others turned their backs.

"Fuck that," added Tom Deakin with feeling.

Arthur held up his hand and said: "Thanks."

The music and dancing started the split second he said: "Thanks" leaving him stranded on the stage holding the microphone.

As he clambered down with it still in hand, it boomed every time he hit the floor. Then, the phrase "God's sake" was clearly heard.

Meanwhile behind closed curtains, Arnold had been festering in his flat. No invite had dropped through his door and he took it personally and despite nobody else getting one, he still felt left out. His boss had done some investigation into his news generating antics and had made it known he was not welcome back. Then the police had been knocking on his front door, but he sat behind it and held his breath.

"We'll call again," he heard the constable say to his colleague. "Next time, we'll bring a sledge hammer." They clearly knew he was in.

Melancholy then set in. He opened the cupboard and found a bottle of last year's sherry. He slumped down and poured a tumbler full. Three tumblers later, after he had chucked up, he had hatched a plan to 'Wipe out the whole frigging village in one go'.

Most of the villagers were in the marquee, so nobody saw Arnold's bedraggled, bruised and limping figure as he crept around the burnt-out remains of the clubhouse. After prizing off the lock, he entered the old store. He struggled in the dim light to see what he was doing. He decided to push open the doors. Between moonlight and streetlight, he could just make out the contour of the ground roller. He had seen the machine started before during a game but never done it himself.

"Can't be that bleeding difficult. Now what did the old git do?" he muttered.

He felt for a lever situated on top of the engine and pushed it forward, turned on the fuel, and then took hold of the clumsy starting handle. His eyes were becoming adjusted to the dark, so he could just make out the hole in the front cover where it should be put. He braced himself, applied pressure, and was surprised at how easy it moved. Faster and faster it turned, without a murmur. Then he recalled the next move. He threw the lever back, but nothing. In the dying moment before it stopped turning, black soot belched from the pepper pot exhaust accompanied by a deafening noise as the motor burst into life. He felt his hair stand on end.

He hoisted himself aboard and gripped the steering wheel. He could see the silhouette of the revellers against the canvas sides of the marquee.

"An easy target," he thought.

His excitement heightened as he pushed the gear lever forward. The machine lurched, then slowly trundled out of the shed. He hysterically waved his arms, as he moved towards the twinkling light of the disco. He had in his mind that it would be swift, like science fiction, that he would zoom across the pitch and destroy all within, then peel away into the distance. But as the roller chugged at its maximum two miles per hour, he had time to consider his actions. Certainly he would kill all inside, but the roller is hardly a getaway car and he could hardly walk let alone run. He quickly counted heads dancing in the tent.

"At least twenty. Life for each one. Be banged up forever."

He squinted and could see the front page. *Key Thrown Away As Killer Locked Up,* he read in his mind.

The closer he got, the more he realised what a mistake it would be. Still under the illusion that he was in control of anything but a 1949 ex-war department road roller, he swung on the steering wheel and applied the brake. Expecting an instant response, he was distressed to feel only a slight drift to the right and not the screeching swerving halt. This put him on a direct course for the means of electrical power for the event, a small generator loaned from the pub. The roller hardly stuttered as it buried the generator deep in the soft turf. What little illumination there was immediately disappeared, plunging the marquee into total darkness. The disco, also powered by the generator, wound down to total silence. The revellers paused momentarily as they heard the throb of the approaching roller, and screamed as they fled out of the tent.

The roller ploughed on through the back of the tent and over the disco equipment. The canvas wrapped itself around Arnold who was now in a blind panic, with his foot firmly pressing down on the accelerator in an effort to escape. The bystanders could only helplessly watch as the roller continued across the pitch with the canvas wrapped round it.

Whether Arnold suffocated prior to being dragged over the top of the roller and buried in the pitch, the coroner could not say. All he did say was: "It would have been a blessing if he had suffocated because it must have been a slow, grisly death."

Newly promoted, Martin was sitting at his desk.

"What do you think Roger?" he said with an air of superiority to his new assistant. *"Cursed Club Claims Another Victim or Nut Rolled And Crushed. It's there somewhere."*

He leaned back on his chair.

"Are you mad or what?" Roger was pulling a facial expression that suggested he was.

"It's what Arnold would have wanted…"

Acknowledgments:
My grateful thanks to Stephanie Hale from the Oxford Literacy
Consultancy for her help and support.